The Rogues' Republic

By G. H. Teed

From No. 85 (New Series (2nd)) March 1927 —Sexton Blake Library.

Stillwoods Edition 2019

Stillwoods.Blogspot.Ca

Catalogue Information:
Title: The Rogues' Republic
Author: G. H. Teed (1886-1938)
Originally from No. 85 (New Series (2nd)) March 1927 —Sexton Blake Library.
Cover illustration adapted from the original by Anon
This Edition by Stillwoods, 2019.
ISBN Canada: 978-1-988304-73-1
Blog: Stillwoods.Blogspot.Ca
Author's Blog: http://ghteed.blogspot.com/
Storefront: http://www.lulu.com/spotlight/lulubook22

A Splendid Tale of Mystery and Intrigue in South America, introducing Dr. Huxton Rymer, Mary Trent, Marie Galante, etc.

When Dr. Huxton Rymer and Mary Trent are travelling to South America, Rymer sees an opportunity for easy money. Once he arrives in Santa Marta, there are at first exotic complications in the form of the Voodoo Queen, Marie Galante, but these are followed by another in the person of Sexton Blake!

REPUBLICAN SWINDLES.
Our Magazine Corner.

The two chief industries of some of the smaller but very quick-living South American States seem to be revolutions and graft. There is something in the air of those republican regions that makes honesty of much less account than sudden wealth— and the rapidity with which fortunes and estates change hands there is startling and staggering.

But not one of those hectic little States has ever pulled off such a gigantic swindle as once set New York screaming for the blood of its political "bosses." It was in connection with Tammany Hall in its notorious stages, when those who ran the ring of crooks who were Tammany Hall—including the then Mayor of New York, one,

Fernando Wood—fairly set that great continent rocking with the enormity of the sums of money which they scooped out of the public purse.

Faked contracts and huge percentages on all contracts given out to firms undertaking work for the Republic were their great stand-by. The story of the rise and fall of that, superbly cheeky and daring ring of crooks is too long to tell here, but the extent of their malpractices, whilst occupying positions of high honour and public trust, can be gauged from one simple fact—that one of the swindlers amassed twelve million dollars in five short years!

More recent times have seen the exposure of an electioneering scandal in Pennsylvania, in which £300,000 was handed out by way of bare-faced bribery by the three contestants for election to a seat in the United States Senate. Workers in the election cause were engaged wholesale, at a rate per hour which made many of them rich for life. They lined up for their pay, at regular intervals, in long queues; and before the pay-out money was fetched from the banks each of the bags containing it were carefully provided with tear-bombs, for the public were beginning to fancy taking a hand in the big game! There was only one correct way of opening the bags of bullion, and many faulty ways, any one of which meant the gassing of the unauthorised swindler!

The Big Republic has another little stunt on hand—at least, its mighty bands of swindlers have. This is the wholesale buying of convicts' releases. The world's newspapers claim for Chicago the ominous title of the world's wickedest city, chiefly on account of the fact that at least ten times as many murders occur in that city as in London. Murderers on purchased parole, and life convicts whom friends have managed to set free after only a few months in gaol, swarm in that city like flies.

Lawyers and M.P.'s are freely accused by the law-abiding citizens of Chicago of asking for, and taking, fees of anything from £200 up to £1000 for securing the unconditional release of prison scum justly condemned to lengthy incarceration by properly impanelled juries. One convict who was unable to raise sufficient "dough" to get his release from prison in this unconventional way declared that the lawyers and others who made this form of swindle their living generally reckoned to have their victims murdered as soon as possible after release, in order that evidence should not be brought against those who worked the illegal liberation.

When a millionaire stood his trial some time ago in the U.S.A. his helpers—a comprehensive word, that!—required a suite of forty rooms in the chief hotel of the town, simply to house them. Apparently the day was to be carried by sheer weight of numbers. But these sensations tread on the heels of one another unceasingly in Uncle Sam's Republic, for shortly after that big affair, one of America's notorious oil-swindlers was run in on a charge involving a £400,000 fraud.

Prohibition accounts for an enormous multitude of astounding exposures in connection with swindling in high places. The unhappy enforcement officers have estimated that 95 per cent of smuggled liquor gets into the country without being spotted, and that profits from the boot-legging business in New York alone tot up to the respectable sum of £720,000,000 a year!

The courts are reckoned to be at least two years in arrears with the trying of cases brought by the prohibition agents, fresh arrests are being made at the rate of about 400 per month. Juries are bribed freely, the heads of the crime trusts and bootlegging gangs hobnob openly with judges—and so America continues to "beat the band" where wholesale and almost unbelievable swindling is concerned.

But Germany has decided not to be outdone. As a young republic, it has much headway to make. Quite a number of successful barristers, and others officially connected with the courts of justice in Berlin, were arrested recently on a charge of trying to push Germany well into the front rank of big republican swindles.

The formal accusation was that they had formed a ring to secure the acquittal of prisoners by the simple "manipulation" of written evidence in the possession of the courts. In the criminal underworld it went by the name of the Acquittal Organisation, on appeal to which—with the necessary backing of big money—any accusative document could be "pinched" from the court archives!

CHAPTER I.   Through the Smoke of a Good Cigar—Huxton Rymer Sees a Red-Headed Youth and Gets a Money-Spinning Idea.

SEVERAL times between Liverpool and Funchal, Huxton Rymer had taken note of the youth with the somewhat, sallow skin and flaming red hair. It was a curious combination, for almost invariably that type of hair is found with a fair, nordic skin.

But no "mop" out of Scotland ever showed more ruddy than that which had caught Rymer's attention, and when the ship had cleared from Madeira for its run across the Western Ocean to the West Indies, the adventurer made it a point to get into conversation with the owner of the hair.

It was not altogether the unusual contrast that had inspired Rymer to strike up an acquaintance with the young man. Rather was it a "something" elusively familiar about the features, more particularly the eyes. Time and again it had struck Rymer that he had seen just such eyes and nose and chin before, but certainly he had never to his knowledge laid eyes on this youth until he saw him on board the Reventazon.

Even with that sallow skin one might have thought the youth to be of some northern race, for the flaming mop was a brand that could not be denied. When one took the trouble to search the passenger list, however, one found that he bore a cognomen of completely Latin origin.

Juan Ruiz de Alarcon Y. Mendoza—that was the name, all of it, just like that.

"Juan Ruiz de Alarcon Y. Mendoza," had mused Rymer when he identified it with the young man who had roused his interest. "I know that name. I'll bet a button! But I didn't know it with all the fixings. Let me see—Juan de Alarcon. No, that isn't it. Ruiz de Alarcon—and that is not it. Ah, hold on my lad, I think I have it—Ruiz Mendoza—just a simple name without the aristocratic 'de' and the family indication of the 'A.' Ruiz Mendoza. Now where the deuce was it that I met him?"

That was one evening just after leaving Funchal, and by the time he had made two rounds of the deck, Rymer had been able to probe back into his memory far enough to dig up the connection he sought.

"Ruiz Mendoza," he murmured, as he saw the youth come out of the saloon and cross to the rail as if to get a breath of air—it was a warm, humid night in September. "I have it now. In other words, Ruiz Mendoza who was one of the must daring freebooters who ever roamed about Spanish America, made a dozen fortunes and lost them, wound up as President, of Santa Marta, and was shot in Cristobal Plaza during the revolution that followed.

"Ruiz Mendoza. That is the bird as sure as little apples grow on trees. And that young follow—twenty-four or so I should say he was—had the same eyes and nose and chin of Don Ruiz, the late lamented president of Santa Marta, or I'm a walleyed salamander. I wonder if by any chance he is his son? If he is, where in the name of Christopher Columbus did he get that head of hair? I think I'll get into conversation with him. One never knows when a tip may turn up."

And so Dr. Huxton Rymer—travelling under his favourite nome de guerre of Professor Andrew Butterfield to the West Indies, ostensibly in search of certain rare lepidoptera—looking not a little distinguished in his well-cut dinner-jacket, and giving the impression of being a man of considerable substance, strolled along the deck in the direction of the young man who, despite his extraordinary red hair, brought back to his mind the Don Ruiz Mendoza he had known some years before.

It was an easy matter for Rymer to pause behind the other and make a casual remark about the closeness of the evening. The young man gave a slight start at the sound of the voice so close to him, then he turned, and, seeing who it was, smiled. He had already taken observation of the fact that this gentleman with the pointed beard had travelling with him an extremely pretty young woman who was known as his niece, and he was by no means blind to the charms of the fair sex. That was one proof of the Spanish blood in him.

There was some desultory conversation, and then, with a smile that excused the somewhat personal nature of the question Rymer asked:

"Are you by any chance related to the late Don Ruiz Mendoza, who was president of Santa Marta? You will excuse the question, I am sure. Your name is similar, but your English is that of an Englishman, so I am puzzled."

Mendoza laughed.

"You are not the first to be puzzled about my appearance and accent, sir," he said pleasantly. "Yes, Don Ruiz was my father. My mother was a Scotch lady, hence my hair. I am really more British than Spanish, for I have not been in Spanish America since I was a kid. My mother brought me away when I was very young. She and my father did not see exactly eye to eye over some of his political doings, and she found the life distasteful."

"I see. It is interesting to meet you. I knew your father well. He was, if you will permit me to say so, a very remarkable man—a great man in many ways. I was with him at the time he gained the presidency of Santa Marta by whipping the Government troops in the plaza. He was the idol of his men."

The young fellow's eyes shone with sudden interest in this man who had known his father. Despite the fact that he had been dragged away from the sanguinary scenes of his father's triumphs at a time when he was helpless to resist, and had not seen his father since, he had made that stormy petrel his hero, and back of his present journey was the desire to meet and know some of the people who had known his father— to learn more about the man of whom his mother had rarely spoken.

It had been a great blow to him that Don Ruiz had been killed a few years before, when he was still at school; it had been the dream of his life to go to him. But this man—this professor who was obviously someone of importance, had known his father, and called him a great man, was an immediate passport to the confidence of young Mendoza.

He opened up at once, and for half any hour poured out every thought and that had filled his life. In that brief time Rymer learned all there was to be known of his history—learned how he had spent his boyhood under the control of a woman who had been more than stern, and who refused all but the smallest morsels of information about his father; learned of the infrequent letters which came to him from that romantic person, and how he treasured them; learned how he had devoted every aim of his education and training to the one ambition—to go out and join his father.

Then came the story of the shock when news had come that President Ruiz Mendoza had been shot dead. He was reticent about how his mother took it, but Rymer could gather that the late filibusterer and the Scotch lady must have had a good many stormy sessions. At any rate, it was plain that the mother had done her best to make the boy forget his father, and bring him up to a conventional life at home; but that the call of the blood had been too strong, and when the last tie had snapped with her death the young man lost no time in making for the scenes where his father had held sway.

"If I had had money of my own I should have gone out a year ago," he wound up, with a slightly embarrassed laugh, as he realised to what an extent he had confided to this stranger; "but I couldn't manage enough capital, so I had to wait until I secured a post. But I am afraid I have bored you. I forget when I get thinking about my father, and you are the first person I have met who knew him in those days."

Rymer smiled again, and flicked the ash from his cigar.

"You have not bored me in any way," he reassured the other. "It is a great pleasure for me to meet the son of Don Ruiz Mendoza. I may say that I played some small part in the affair of the plaza at Santa Marta. I was with him for weeks, and he confided many of his most secret hopes to me. He spoke often of his wife in England, and of his son. That would be you. It was the great hope of his heart, I am sure, that one day you come out to him. And now that you are bound for that country what are you going to do?"

"My rôle is a very small one compared to my father's. I am not going to Santa Marta now, although I hope to make it before long. I am going out to Costa Rica as a wireless operator for the Amalgamated Fruit Company. They have a big station there in connection with their banana fleet."

"I know it well," rejoined Professor Butterfield, though he did not take the trouble to explain under just what circumstances he was last in Costa Rica. "We must talk again of your father."

"Indeed we must!" exclaimed the other. "I am eager to have you tell me more about him if you will, sir. Are you travelling to Santa Marta now, may I ask?"

Rymer waved his cigar expressively.

"We—my niece and I—are going to the West Indies and the Main. I cannot tell you just what our plans are. We shall wander as the fancy takes us. I am in search of some rare lepidoptera which I hope to find among some of the lesser islands. It is quite possible that you may see us in Costa Rica. My colleagues, Barnes and Webber, brought back very interesting specimens last year, but the field is quite untouched yet. And here comes my niece now. Do you dance?"

Young Mendoza assured him that he did, and in a few moments

he was being presented to Mary Trent. In making the introduction, her "uncle" made the slightest significant signal with one eyelid, which Mary had no difficulty in interpreting. Immediately she was shyly gracious to the young man, and by the time he led her away to dance on the other side of the deck, he was being handled exactly as Rymer wished. When Mary Trent took the trouble, she could be a most devastating person with harder nuts than Ruiz Mendoza.

It was not, however, until somewhat later that Mary learned why Rymer had wished her to throw the net of her charm about the young man. After hanging about as long as he decently could, he had taken himself off to the smoke-room, and then, alone in a secluded part of the deck, where Mary was keeping her "uncle" company while he finished his cigar, Rymer told her why he had picked up an acquaintance with the other.

"I spotted him at once, my dear," he said in a low tone. "I have had my eye on him ever since we left Liverpool. There was something about his features that was familiar, and yet, I couldn't quite place what it was. Of course, it was the red hair that did it. If he had had black hair I would have known for certain he must be a near relative of Ruiz Mendoza. And the best of it is, I did know old Ruiz intimately. In fact, we were in more than one little affair together. But, in the son's eyes, the old rascal could do no wrong. I played on that string!"

"But why? In what way can he be of use to us? It will have to be something that has considerable promise, for I assure you I do not find it agreeable to bring him to heel. He is, I suspect, a very impressionable young man where my sex is concerned."

Rymer grinned.

"So much the better. He won't feel the burn so badly when he learns the truth. But you must play him for the present, Mary. I have an idea we may turn that young man to our financial use in some way."

"You have no definite plan?"

"Not yet. But look at the material. The son of Don Ruiz Mendoza! He hasn't set foot yet in Santa Marta, where his father was president. Despite his rascality old Don Ruiz was a personality, and there are a good many people in Santa Marta who would follow him if he were alive today. The son is bound to find a big following if he ever goes to the country. And with politics always in a state of flux, why—well, I might think up something."

"But he told me he was going to Costa Rica as a wireless operator."

"He thinks he is, and maybe he is. But I can tell you now, my dear girl, that if I can hit on anything that promises well, he will not go to Costa Rica. The voyage is young yet and for once in a way we are not pinched for cash to swing something if it offers."

Mary laid a small hand on his arm. "You can't keep away from it can you?" she murmured. "I stand with you in whatever it is, only don't risk all."

"Don't worry, Mary. We will dole out every penny piece as if it was a sovereign. But, I have a hunch there ought to be some good hunting down in this part of the world, just now. It hasn't been worked for some time past, and I have the glimmering of an idea—a peach of an idea, my dear. If I can work it out the right way, there ought to be a big prospect in it. If there is, that young man will never see Costa Rica. If there isn't—well, no harm will be done."

And so Mary left him to smoke and spin his schemes until he was the last one on deck. That his mind was at work on something Mary knew, for the following day he renewed his association with young Mendoza, and made occasion for the young man to be placed full in the range of Mary's fascination. Mary, to whom the whole thing was a game in which she went unscathed, developed several new methods of attack—they really appeared more as barriers of defence, which the youth grew more and more avid to scale—which made Rymer wag his head approvingly. As a result, Mendoza was completely enslaved long before they reached Bridgetown.

It is no exaggeration to say, that if Mary had asked him to turn a somersault off the deck in Bridgetown harbour, he would have done so in full view of all the blacks. But Mary was too clever a little artist for that. Time and again she brought him up to a pitch when she was forced to slip away in order to avoid a passionate outburst. She had no great qualms about the part she was playing, for her instinct was right. Mendoza was, as she had told Rymer, extremely susceptible, and Mary knew there would be no lasting scars when the thud came. It was not that he had not the capacity for deep affection. He possessed that all right, but Mary knew that his craze for her was more infatuation for her chic prettiness and her alluring smile than anything else.

She had an idea a very different type of girl would reach his inmost being, and later on she was to prove that instinct right as well. There was no risk of Mary suffering, for all that she possessed had long ago been given to Rymer. He was the only thing that mattered to her, and although her coming into his life had not caused him to desert his old paths, she had had, nevertheless, an influence for good on him.

She was willing to be his partner in any scheme he proposed, so long as it was within certain limits she had set her self; and it is a fact that, since having Mary with him, Rymer had developed a finesse of play which had been dormant before.

As soon as they were away from Barbados, Rymer brought his full battery into play. In this sort of thing he was a past master. Even without Mary's influence he had brought young Mendoza into a mood of receptiveness which was ideal for the seed he had to sow. So quietly but persistently had he played on his aforetime friendship with the defunct Don Ruiz, that Mendoza now looked upon him as his greatest friend. With his infatuation added to that, plus a naturally romantic temperament, he was ripe for the proposals which Rymer had ready.

It was when Barbados was out of sight on the starboard quarter, and they were running down between Grenada and Tobago, that Rymer chose his moment. A lovely warm evening, with a waxing moon over the tropic sea, had enabled Mary to get in some devastating work as a preliminary. Then, as they paced the deck later, Rymer inserted the thin edge of the wedge.

"It was just such a night as this that we rode into the plaza at Santa Marta," he said dreamily. "I shall never forget it; one moment the town was silent in slumber, the next the whole place was in an uproar, with your father at the head of it all, and the multitude hailing him as 'el presidente.'" He sighed heavily. "What talk for a staid professor to indulge in, but I would give much if those days were back again. To have the right to claim a position such as that, and to be able to fight for it is the sort of thing that makes life worth while. And your father had the right even as you would have it if you had ever chosen to exercise it."

Mendoza turned to him eagerly.

"I have thought often of that, sir," he said, with a new throb in his voice. "I would give anything if I had been old enough to take my place beside my father. In one of his letters to me, which I managed to see, he said that, he hoped one day I, too, should sit in the presidential chair of Santa Marta,"

"Well, why not—why not?" murmured Rymer, as if more to himself than the other.

The young man laughed shortly.

"What a hope! I have neither money nor influence. I am just a poor wireless operator, in whom nobody is interested."

Rymer might have made some sly remark about Mary just then, but he forbore. He knew her work was proving quite effective without any assistance from him.

"You are mistaken in one thing, my boy. You are not without friends and, knowing what I do, I am quite sure a great many people in Santa Marta would gladly acclaim the son of the redoutable Don Ruiz Mendoza. I am willing to go further and say that if you were to aspire to the presidency of the country, you would have every chance of winning it."

For a few moments golden visions filled the other's mind. He saw himself at the head of an army marching into Santa Marta with the people huzzaing and acclaiming him on every side; he saw himself in all the panoply of state seated on the president's chair, while uniformed ministers filed past him. And he could not eliminate from the picture the dainty form of Mary Trent, who fitted into the colourful dream so perfectly. It was just the vision that any other young fellow of his temperament would have had.

He drew a deep breath.

"That—that is not for me," he said at last huskily. "I might have had a chance if my father had lived, but now—"

Rymer paused at the rail and lit a fragrant Sobranie cigarette. He gave one to his companion, then he gazed at the latter in serious contemplation.

"Do you know," he said slowly and impressively, "your words cause me to think seriously. It is true your father is gone, but I, his close friend, remain. Why should I not make you my protege? Why should I not stand behind you in a claim which you have a perfect right to make? I am a scientist from choice not from necessity. I am, if I may say so without appearing boastful, possessed of considerable private means. I am therefore in a position to finance your claim. Don Ruiz Mendoza the second, President of the glorious Republic of Santa

Marta! How does that sound? Why shouldn't you take up your father's work where he left off? You have the benefit of cautious, Scotch blood in your veins, and an English education. But by birth you are a citizen of Santa Marta. You have every claim to the presidential chair. Your words have inspired me to see great possibilities. By thunder, my boy,"—and here he laid a hand on the other's shoulder —"I'll back you to the limit if you want to have a shot at it. Instead of being a wireless operator in Costa Rica, you can become President of Santa Marta. Think it over, my boy, and if you have the nerve and ambition, hanged if I don't put you in that chair, as sure as your father ever sat in it. Say no more to-night. Sleep on the idea, and to-morrow we will talk it over—the three of us, you, my niece, and I."

And Rymer was wise enough to leave it at that just then. The bait had been cast and the fish showed every sign of swallowing it.

CHAPTER 2. Rymer Continues His Spinning Until They Reach Santa Marta—An Unexpected Encounter Follows, which Opens Up New Possibilities and Complications.

BY the time the Reventazon had left the Windward Islands behind and was nosing through the Leewards, Juan Ruiz de Alarcon y Mendoza had definitely abandoned his post in Costa Rica and had thrown himself heart and soul into the alluring scheme which Rymer had so cunningly woven. Even Lady Luck herself seemed to be sitting in at the game for the one thing that stood in the way of Mendoza leaving the ship at Santa Marta was his contract with the company in Costa Rica. Here is where the goddess of Chance produced another young man on board who was a qualified wireless operator on the lookout for a job. He was making for the Panama Canal, where he had hoped to pick up something. A little use of the wireless and the matter was arranged. Evans, the other youth, was only too pleased at getting the job, while Mendoza was free to go ashore with Rymer and Mary Trent.

During the few days between Barbados and Dos Hermanos (which was the port for Santa Marta) Rymer put in a busy time planning what the next step should be when they got ashore. He had one definite idea in his mind—to make use of young Mendoza in some way to plot an upheaval in Santa Marta. He was sufficiently au fait with the current history of that turbulent republic to know that almost any time was ripe for a revolution, and he figured he had a strong card to play in Mendoza.

Before making any big move, however, it would be necessary for him to sound the opposition to the government after landing, for his own game would be strengthened materially if he could persuade them to come in with him. That was where Mendoza would come forward.

He said nothing of this to the youth. And as for Mendoza, now that he had burned his bridges he was leaving himself entirely in the hands of Rymer and Mary Trent. It was perhaps as well for Rymer, that no one on board recognised the adventurer in the grave-faced professor. A hint to Mendoza might have spoilt things, but then Rymer spent most of his life in taking chances, and once he got the ball rolling well he didn't much care if Mendoza did discover his identity. He would be in too deep by then to draw out even if he

10

wanted to. Once get him actually committed—that was Rymer's aim.

Mary handled the young fellow in masterly fashion until he had been safely shepherded into the Pension Inglesa in Santa Marta. There had been a few moments risk during scrutiny of passports at Dos Hermanos, but with Mendoza's wedged in between Rymer's and Mary's, a careless inspector had been more interested in the money which Rymer slipped into his palm than in the names on the passports.

Therefore, Don Juan Ruiz de Alarcon y Mendoza, son of the famous president Don Ruiz Mendoza, returned to his people unheralded and unknown. At the hotel he was registered under his mother's name as a matter of precaution, and with that first step safely accomplished, Rymer set about the next.

This was to secure reliable information as to the present political condition of the country. Rymer knew his way about Santa Marta well enough, even if it had been a few years since he had been there. He knew which cafes and wine shops were invariably anti-government no matter which side was in, and it was among those he knew he would pick up the clue he was after.

With this in his mind, he sent Mendoza off with Mary Trent. Mary could keep him employed in the big cathedral; where in the cool, dim chapels there was plenty to detain him in the history of the country. In the meantime, Rymer started off to make his round of the cafes and wine shops.

He had one particular place in mind which he had known well in the past. It was in a narrow, dusty street not far from the plaza—the same Cristobal plaza where Don Ruiz Mendoza had been shot, and as he went along in the blitzing glare of the early afternoon, Rymer saw that the sanitary arrangements had not been improved since his last visit.

The open drain still ran down the centre of the street, which at that hour of the day was devoid of human beings other than Rymer. His only companions, as it were, consisted of the zopolodis (carrion birds) which strutted impudently about searching for offal. Every window was shuttered, and behind those shutters the more sober citizen took siesta.

At the end of the street was the wine shop which Rymer had in mind. It was a place of villainous aspect, backing on to a wharf that jutted out into the yellow delta of the stream on which Santa Marta stood. Nominally, San Jose, in the interior, was the capital of the republic, but the wealth was in Santa Marta on the coast and it was there that governments were made and unmade.

Three miles down that yellow stream was the small, dirty port of Dos Hermanos, where they had landed. Shipping would have come right in to Santa Marta itself were it not for the existence of sandbars at the mouth of the delta which made this impossible.

Rymer swung into the wine shop without hesitation. At first he could see nothing, coming in from the terrific glare of the street into the dim interior of the shop. He paused just inside, waiting until his pupils should accommodate themselves to the gloom, and it was while he stood thus that he became aware of an altercation going on in the back room which, he remembered, opened off the front shop with no door to block the way—just an opening in the thin wooden partition.

One voice he recognised at once as the throaty burr of an island negro; the other was in the lighter pitch of the coast mongrel or mestizo. And from the scraps that reached his ears, he soon discovered that the argument had evidently come up during the course of a game of cards. He moved along past the rough counter, pushed aside some small tables and chairs which, at that hour, were unpatronised, and stood looming in the doorway which gave into the back room. The only light came through a small barred opening through which Rymer could see the yellow swirl of water beyond the end of the short wharf.

At his appearance, the two who were quarrelling on either side of a round table paused and regarded the newcomer. They were held speechless by the sight, for it was decidedly unusual to see a white-clad European in such a place at any time, much less during the hot hours of the afternoon.

But the truce lasted only for a moment. Convinced that this stranger was some accidental bird of passage they went at it again, and Rymer's eyes flickered as he saw the negro, a giant half-naked specimen with the cut of Martinique about him, cover the table in one magnificent leap.

The smaller mestizo should have been there; but he wasn't. With the speed of a panther he sidestepped, and the driving knife that should have found his heart went hurtling against the soft wood of a bench. The negro let out a blood-curdling oath, and for one moment the slanting light from the window fell on his eyes.

That momentary glimpse was enough for Huxton Rymer. The black was about to run amok, he knew, and scarcely had he time to grasp this when, forgetting the mestizo, the negro clawed another knife from under the dirty cotton bags which were his solo article of clothing and came straight at the big European.

Huxton Rymer knew better than to argue with a man when he was amok. He had handled such cattle in too many ports of the world to try any method except one —to get the crazy fool before he got him. And now, with a speed that matched that shown by the mestizo, he jumped to one side just as the knife blade whistled past his shoulder. In the same moment there came the slam of a door, and from the gloom of a corner a low, liquid voice came to him—the voice of a woman in urgent warning.

Rymer took one fleeting look towards the corner whence the voice had come. In that brief instant he was only able to register on the retina the imprssion of something whitish, blurred in the gloom. Then he needed all his attention for the negro.

With such violence had the latter driven the blade towards his intended victim that the point had been driven clean through the thin wooden partition, and was protruding on the other side. Still clinging to the handle the black was, perforce, held as it were, and it was while he stood thus, struggling to drag the steel out of the wood, that Huxton Rymer came into action.

He drove in his right fist with a force and precision that caught the negro just under the ear. It was an ox-felling blow, and not even that husky Martinique could stand up under it. He lurched sideways, and realising even through the haze of his drink mania that something of altogether exceptional force was up against him he released his hold on the knife.

He found the wall with his back, and crouched like some jungle beast, peering through white-rimmed eyes to see just what it was. In his former delirium he had been plunging recklessly, wildly, unseeingly. Rymer's jolt had done more than anything else to bring him to his senses.

But Huxton Rymer knew that the black must not have time to recover. Only a severe punishment would settle him, and so, with both arms going like steel pistons, he went in.

Thud! Thud! Thud!

In that small room the blows sounded terrific against the wide barrel of the negro's torso. And again:

Thud! Thud! Thud!

The woman in the corner gasped at the sound. Had there been light enough one might have seen a savage gleam of admiration in her eyes as she watched the big white man in action. As for the mestizo he was clinging to the table, his eyes goggling in stupefaction at the spectacle. He still couldn't quite understand how it was this stranger had appeared in the nick of time. If he had not done so he well knew the point of the blade would have found his heart in the negro's second mad rush.

A slight change came in the timbre of the blows.

Crack! Crack!

Just like that—twice. Rymer had shifted the direction of his onslaught. At first he had been tattooing the solar plexus, but despite the terrific force of the blows, the negro's stomach muscles had withstood them. He was breathing heavily and groaning with sharp agony, but he was beginning to recover, and Rymer knew he must end it soon if at all. Therefore, he changed his position a little, and suddenly sent in a couple of terrific "haymakers."

Crack! Crack!

A hard right to the jaw, and, as the black's head went back against the wall with a thud that would have smashed an ordinary skull, Rymer let loose his left. It connected exactly on the point, sending the negro down side ways as if a mule had kicked him. He flopped over once, tried to rise, then slumped again, and this time lay still.

Rymer stood back, panting heavily. It had been strenuous exercise for such a hot afternoon, and he was no lover of violent action except at moments of his own choosing. He had forgotten the mestizo entirely, but now he found that individual dancing about him, pouring out protestations of gratitude and calling all his favourite saints to witness that he was forever more the servant of his rescuer.

Rymer brushed him aside and advanced to meet the woman who was moving towards him. They met just a foot or so away from the barred window, and then as he saw her features plainly for the first time Rymer gave a low exclamation of amazement. It was no stranger that he was gazing upon, but a woman whom he knew well—one with whom his life had been intimately associated in the past.

It was none other than Marie Galante, the Mystery Woman of

Hayti, the Voodoo Queen of all the blacks among the isles of the Caribbean!

CHAPTER 3. Rymer Spins a New Thread Into His Scheme— Marie Galante Also Turns Spinner.

THE recognition had been mutual. The mulatto woman, still as lithe and exotic as of old, as he could see, caught him by the white sleeve of his coat and peered up at him, her eyes languorously alight with that hungry jungle look which Rymer knew so well.

"You?" he whispered. "It is—you. How do you come here?"

Rymer knew she was thinking of the last time they had been together in New York— on the occasion when Marie Galante had gone north to fish in the turgid pool of the black life of New York, and had lured to his ruin the powerful negro, who was known as the Black Emperor. Chance had thrown Rymer into that same game, and through him, Marie Galante had betrayed the Black Emperor. Little had she gained from it all, for in the moment when Sexton Blake had smashed the whole black organisation to bits and had sent Rymer and Marie Galante fleeing for safety Rymer had broken with her, coldly and brutally, drawn back to England by the influence of Mary Trent.

He was wondering what she would have to say when she learned—as she must—that this girl whose existence had made her frantically jealous before was actually here with him in Santa Marta. He began to feel just then that perhaps his inspiration regarding young Mendoza had not been such a lucky one after all. But there was no turning back now, and with his usual cool insouciance Rymer met the challenge of her eyes.

"We shall talk presently," he said. "But first what about that?" And he indicated the unconscious negro.

The mulatto woman made a gesture of contempt, and laid a small automatic pistol on the table.

"The carrion! I was ready to shoot him. Throw him out on to the wharf. I shall deal with him later."

Rymer signed to the mestizo to give him a hand, and, between them they dragged the negro out through a door, and heaved him down some wooden steps to the wharf. The mestizo then disappeared, and Rymer re-entered the wine shop to deal with the woman.

She was busy in the front shop when he closed the door, but called to him to wait, and presently she reappeared, bringing with her a bottle of wine and two glasses. She sat down by the table, motioning to him to do likewise; then, when she had filled the glasses and lighted a cigarette, she gazed at him through half-closed lids.

"Well?"

Rymer pledged her in the wine, and put a match to one of his own Sobranios. He was jockeying for a time; the woman knew it, and Rymer knew that she knew it. He was perfectly aware that Marie Galante, with all her power among the blacks of the West Indies and the Spanish Main, would not be spending her time in that dingy wine shop in Santa Marta unless she had some strong reason for doing so. It was quite on the cards that she was mixed up in some political intrigue in Santa Marta. If so, then this circumstance would complicate his own plans considerably. If he could bend her forces to his will it might prove a very strong advantage. If she lined up as an enemy then, he knew, his case would be pretty well hopeless.

Any scheme must include the support of the riff-raff of the coast country, and Marie Galante directed every movement of that class. If he had been alone the matter would have been simple. For all her guile and cunning she was a woman, and a woman who had nursed a strong passion for Huxton Rymer for some years. How he could explain Mary Trent was the big problem, and again, how Mary would regard this exotic creature of the jungle was still more problematical.

He took the plunge in his usual manner. He smiled as if he had nothing at all to conceal as far as possible, to avoid any mention of what had taken place in New York.

"You ask me how it is I am in Santa Marta," he said easily. "That is easily explained. I just drifted in, though, to be quite frank, I have a certain scheme in my mind. But you—what are you doing here? This wine shop is an odd sort of place to find you."

She studied him for a few moments in silence; then she shrugged.

"I don't know whether you are lying or not," she muttered. "But I'll find out. You ask me what I am doing here. I will tell you, though there is no reason why I should. There are—pickings in Santa Marta these days; and there are reasons why I do not wish to be among the islands at present. This wine shop is, as you must know, if you know Santa Marta, the very centre of all the coast intrigue. It is useful to me."

"I can quite understand that. You say there are 'pickings.' Do you mean political?"

"I may answer that later. I want first to hear more about you, I have not very pleasant recollections of the way in which you acted in

New York."

Rymer lifted a deprecatory hand.

"Please," he said, "you know I could do nothing else at the time. It was better that we should take different ways—the pursuit was too hot."

The disturbing scent of her came to him as she leant across towards him.

"I did more for you than I have ever done for any other living being," she panted. "I had the Black Emperor as I have never had any slave; I had millions in my hand, and yet I threw everything away for you. Can anything ever explain that? Do you think I am to be satisfied with empty words? What did I care if Sexton Blake had made things too hot for us?

"Do you think we couldn't have settled him quickly enough if we had lured him to the West Indies? There isn't an island, there isn't a cay in the whole archipelago where he could walk in safety if I but lifted my hand. You know it, and you know it was not fear of him that caused you to break away. Don't hand me empty words, for here, even in Santa Marta, I am among my people—the people who do anything— anything when I lift a finger. I am willing to listen—now; to-morrow I may not do so. Why are you in Santa Marta? When did you come? I want the truth."

Rymer shifted a little uneasily. He had expected protests, but not such a tirade as this. She was in a mood where a slight thing would send her completely off the deep end. He was going to need a good deal of finesse just then, and he realised it. But Huxton Rymer had a way with him when he wanted to employ it.

"You are being unfair to me," he said gently and in a slightly aggrieved tone. "If you will reflect a little I think you will acknowledge that I could do no different in New York than I did. We were short of funds, and didn't know which way to turn. Sexton Blake, with half the police of New York, was on our heels. I did give you nearly all the money and made sure that you were safe before I thought of myself."

Her eyes softened a little. She was beginning to feel the spell that had always "got" her, if one may use the word.

"I don't deny that. But you didn't come with me. You knew you would have been all right once we reached the islands."

"I know—I know; but I should have been a handicap to you. It wouldn't have been fair. You needed a chance to turn round. The only thing for me to do was to take a separate line. I have always fought on my own, and I always shall."

She admitted the truth of this, and when Rymer laid one hand on hers she was willing to listen to reason. At the same time, her curiosity was far from satisfied, and she was no less a power to be reckoned with than she had been a few minutes before.

"What has brought you to Santa Marta?" she persisted. "Are you alone?"

Again Rymer edged. It wasn't time yet, he had to know more.

"I am not exactly alone," he temporised. "And I will tell you everything presently. But I want to know first about you. What is afoot? Why are you hidden away here in this wine shop? Are you known in the place? And is it something political?"

She nodded.

"There is a good deal. I have been here for nearly three months I came down from Hayti. Santa Marta is full of unrest, and there will be a revolution here before long. It has been brewing for a long time, but they lacked two things— competent leadership and money. I have supplied both."

Rymer looked thoughtful. If what she said was true then it was plain that she was going to be a very big factor in his own schemes. If he could not win her as an ally then he would be up against a tough proposition. On the other hand she could not have a more suitable candidate than he could produce.

"You mean you are organising the opposition?"

"Yes. There is a good deal of intrigue up in San Jose. There always has been, but for a long time past it has been getting thicker. The state finances are in a rotten condition. Everyone in the government is stealing as fast and as hard as he can. I suppose you know that the state has just repudiated the interest on its last foreign loan."

"Yes, I read of that some days ago."

"Well, this is the third year running that it has happened. English and American financial interests have complained, and I know that a warning has been received from the United States that the government must put its house in order. It can't do that; the rot has gone too far. Therefore, it is a good time to strike. With another government in power don't you see the possibilities?"

"I certainly do. A new government—a new loan on the promise that all back interest will be paid up—and the balance goes into the pockets of the government. Doesn't that state the case?"

For the first time since he had entered the wine shop Marie Galante smiled.

"You have stated it perfectly. And now —you?"

"Would you be surprised to know that I have come to Santa Marta on exactly the same errand?"

"Nothing about you would surprise me. What is your scheme?"

"You said a few minutes ago that the revolutionary party here had lacked a leader and money until you came. I can understand how you could supply those deficiencies, but you can't very well run as president."

"Of course not."

"Then who is your candidate? I know this country well enough to be quite sure that whatever his character only some died-in-the-wool son of the state would do."

"Quite so. I have one, although he isn't all that one might desire. It is General Primo de Miguel, who was Secretary for War in a former government. He has been a candidate for the presidency three times, and was banished after the last election. I picked him up in Jamaica before coming here."

"Which means that he must remain in hiding until the hour strikes?"

"Yes; but that is not far distant."

"Would, it interest you if I told you I could produce a candidate who has no drawbacks and, on the contrary, would appeal mightily to the imagination of the people?"

"Do you mean yourself?"

"No; I said before that the candidate on this occasion would have to be a native Santa Martan. I have one—in fact, it was the possession of this candidate, so to say, that inspired my plan."

"Who is he?"

"You have heard, of course, of the late president of Santa Marta—Don Ruiz Mendoza?"

"Yes. If Mendoza were alive there would be no chance in this place for us. He had the whole country in the hollow of his hand."

"Not quite all; don't forget he was shot right here in the plaza. But that need not be discussed now. Would you consider Mendoza's son as a likely candidate?"

"His son! I didn't know he had one. Are you joking?"

In her sudden interest she had bent forward eagerly, and Rymer knew that his card was even stronger than he had hoped.

"I am not joking. Mendoza married a Scotswoman. They didn't agree. The woman left him and went to England, taking with her the only son. She tried to throttle off all the father's influence, but enough crept through for the boy to make him his hero and long to follow in his steps.

"When the mother died the boy was free, and now he is in my care, pledged to do just as I say. I have brought him to Santa Marta—he is in the city now, and he is the next president of Santa Marta. I can see great difficulties if we work separately, but I can see a strong prospect of success if we join forces.

"You have done a lot of preliminary organising work, but there is no denying that my candidate will have the whole country for him if the cards are played properly. What do you say? Do we run this thing as partners? I am willing to dicker on any reasonable basis."

Her lithe body twisted like that of a serpent as she bent closer to him. Her eyes were heavy with the flow of the wine and the surge of her thoughts. The jungle creature in her was once more ready to fawn on this man who had held her and spurned her.

"Come again this evening," she murmured. "We will talk again then. But I think we shall work together."

Which meant that, for the moment, the game was in Rymer's hands. And just then he put aside the thought that this same creature who was just now nothing but yielding tenderness, anxious to accede to his wishes, could become a tornado of fury more dangerous to handle than a cartload of dynamite.

For Mary Trent had still to be explained.

CHAPTER 4. While Huxton Rymer and Marie Galantc Spin Their Scheme on the Coast Certain Incidents which are Fated to Affect Some of Them Considerably are Taking Place in San Jose.

ON the evening before Rymer landed in Santa Marta, and thus before he had had his preliminary conversation with the Voodoo Queen, Marie Galante, certain events were in course up in San Jose which were bound to have a considerable influence on their intrigues, although, even if they had known of them, they would have found it impossible then to see any connection.

As has already been explained, San Jose is purely a nominal capital of the republic. It possesses a smaller population and far less wealth than the port of Santa Marta, its chief importance being that the parliament buildings are situated there, and it is a much pleasanter place of residence than the coast town. When sufficient government funds can leak through the fingers of the grafters to extend the railway from where it putters out some thirty miles from San Jose, then the capital will come into its own. But until then it is doomed to be forced to rest content with the empty glory of being called the capital, of cradling the aristocracy of the country and of boasting of its university while the coast town gathers in the shekels and revels in intrigue.

It is a pleasant little place set some six thousand feet up in the Sierras and its public buildings are excellent. They were built at a time when the spirit of Simon Bolívar still hovered over the land, and men of some degree of honesty were at the head of the government. In the main plaza, and the short boulevards which lead off it, there has been some effort to maintain the buildings and streets in some degree of care; but once one wanders away from that centre one finds nothing but narrow mean streets, as malodorous as any in the low coast town.

On the night before Huxton Rymer landed in Santa Marta, two figures, having the appearance of low-class peons, issued forth from a small adobe hut in one of these streets. They were in sharp physical contrast, for one was tall and broad of shoulder while the other was short and stocky. Yet both revealed a type of bodily strength and vigour of movement which was lacking in the average native.

Their garments were of the scantiest. A pair of loose pants made of the coarse weave of the country, loose flannel shirts and sombreros of soft felt, much less expansive than the Mexican variety, was all that

22

was visible. Each wore a woollen vest beneath the flannel shirt and woollen drawers under the pants, for the nights at that altitude can be distinctly chilly even if the equator does run within four degrees to the south. They wore neither socks nor shoes, their feet being quite bare as those of the lower class peon. Shoes are a luxury which only the comparatively well-to-do can run to.

There was one article of equipment, however, which was as invisible as the underwear referred to which each carried, and which was certainly rarely to be found among the possessions of a common peon. That was a very modern automatic pistol, the clip of which was jammed to the full with cartridges. The weapon of the peon is a knife, but then these two were not natives of San Jose. They had been occupying the hut for only a week; and the few persons to whom they had spoken understood that they had come across the border from the neighbouring republic.

What their business was in San Jose they gave no hint, but it was generally understood that they were making for the emerald mines of Colombia, where they hoped to find employment. It would have surprised their neighbours considerably if they had known that the couple had been living a surprising type of double life since they had come to San Jose—that when they sallied forth each morning it was only to make for a certain house at the opposite side of the town there to change into the clothes of the type worn by the Santa Martan clerk class—similar, but less well cut than those of Europeans.

This was but the first step in their duties of each day. When the pair again appeared in the streets they were sufficiently like others abroad to attract no attention, and, in the finance department of the treasury where they were employed, it was understood that the elder of the two was an accountant from Panama, who had had training with the Canal Corporation in modern methods of accounting, and had been brought to San Jose by Don Fernando Alvarez, the Minister of Finance, in order to introduce, if possible, a less cumbersome system than was at present in vogue.

The younger was known as his assistant. And since the elder, Senor Ramon Castro, was regarded as but a temporary official, who could not possibly have his eye on any permanent departmental plum, he was tolerated without jealousy by the regular staff at the treasury. The lad, to their minds, did not count.

There would have been considerable flitterings in that particular dovecot, and no little consternation, had the regulars dreamed for a single moment that Senor Ramon Castro, accountant of Panama, and, it was understood, a Venezuelan by birth, was none other than Sexton Blake, the famous English criminologist, while the youth who worked with him was his almost equally famous assistant, Tinker.

Just why Sexton Blake and Tinker were in San Jose will be evident as this record of one of Blake's greatest cases is unfolded.

On this night, however, they did not go as usual to the other side of the town to change their clothes. Instead they made direct for the plaza, and from there worked round to the back of the treasury building— a big well-constructed edifice standing by itself in a thickly grown place of crotons and royal palms.

During the week or so they had been at work in the department they had taken careful note of all the arrangements, and knew that, in the ordinary course, there should be not more than the usual nightly guard of six soldiers on the outside. These, they had learned, were placed three at the back and three in front, the two end guards in each instance making a beat round the end of the building to meet the man from the opposite side. There was a shorter central beat front and back which one man performed, meeting each end man alternately.

Inside the building there was one man on duty, a nignt-watchman who was supposed to perambulate the place at regular intervals during the night. Whether he did so or not was yet to be discovered.

Their objective that night was nothing less than the private bureau allotted to the president of the republic. And in order to reach it they had first to get past the outer guards before dealing with the man inside. Even if they succeeded in accomplishing this, they had a difficult task to perform before making a retreat.

It had taken several days of careful survey of the buildings to pick on a weak spot that would fulfil the conditions which must exist if they were to elude the guards. This spot was a window in a sort of semi-basement which Blake had at last fixed on as offering the most chance. It opened into a lumber-room of sorts where old books and papers were kept, and from this there was a passage which connected with several other rooms on the same level before ending in a flight of stairs which led to the main ground floor.

That afternoon Tinker had managed to make his way to the lumber-room and press back the catch of the sash. If the watchman had taken note of this they would probably find it relocked, but, judging from the slackness of the average Santa Martan they did not deem this very likely.

Just outside the window was a sort of small area or well to permit light to enter, although the upper part of the window was above the level of the ground. In this small space there was just about room for them to crouch in the shadow providing they first got past the guards at the back.

They reached the street behind the gardens without attracting any attention. They were exactly similar in appearance to the great bulk of those who were abroad, and no notice was taken of the couple that lounged along the almost deserted street which ran at the back of the public buildings. Blake touched the lad's arm as they came abreast of a giant allamanda tree. The wide-spreading branches thickly grown with huge bluish-purple leaves hung out over the iron spikes of the fence which had been set in the low stone wall separating the grounds of the treasury from the road. Under that canopy they were completely invisible, and, after a swift look up and down the street, Blake gave the lad a leg up.

By using both spikes and one of the branches, Tinker managed to get into the tree where he clung, waiting for Blake. The latter was up with scarcely a sound, and then after a whispered caution to the lad began to work his way forward until he was well inside the fence. A soft hiss brought Tinker after him, and then the two clung like giant sloths while they listened for the footsteps of the guard.

The back of the treasury building was now less than twenty yards away, but even though there were brilliant stars overhead they could not make out its bulk. The leaves of the allamanda were too thick, and the intervening shrubs too closely grown for their eyes to pierce the screen.

But they caught the sound of voices and after listening closely Blake decided they came from the direction of the building and not from the street. He touched the lad on the shoulder, drawing him closer.

"Two of them are talking," he breathed. "They are on the job all right—only thing to do is to try and sneak past them. I am going to swing down to the ground. You come after me—dangle your legs, and I will guide you."

Tinker breathed a "Right-ho, guv'nor," and Blake shifted out a little on the branch. As he did so he felt it bend downwards under his

25

weight. But he had little fear of it breaking, for he knew the wood of the allamanda to be tough and resilient. Out still further he crept until the branch bowed under him in a precipitous arc. Then Blake felt for a firm hold and allowed his legs to swing clear. The lurch of his body carried the branch down still farther, and when he let go he found he had only a foot or so to drop into soft turf.

He stood a little to one side and waited. Tinker's coming was heralded by his swinging feet which almost caught Blake in the face. The detective shot out his hands and gripped the lad's ankles. Tinker let go, and a moment later was standing beside his master.

"Slip your finger inside my belt and keep close," whispered Blake. "I am going to work my way over to the path at the back of the building."

Tinker obeyed, and after listening for a few moments Blake began to steal forward. There was no lack of cover, and he took advantage of it. Even if it had been moonlight only a very sharp eye constantly on the alert would have spotted those two shadows, linked together, stealing across the garden. Blake was a past master at that sort of game, and he had trained Tinker well.

When he paused at last behind the shelter of a huge Amazonian croton close to the edge of the gravelled path they were less than a dozen feet from the steps at the back of the building, and only twenty feet or so from the little well which was their next objective.

But the guards had yet to be circumvented. The murmur of voices still came from somewhere in the gloom indicating that two if not all three of the guards at the rear were gossiping. As far as Blake could make out they were near the broad steps, and, knowing the native as he did, he realised it was quite possible they might idle there half the night before moving.

Blake did not know when, if at all, an officer made the rounds, but he did know the early guard was changed at midnight. There was a certain amount of movement about the building at that time, and he wished, if possible, to get the job he had to do finished before then.

The thing that had to be accomplished first, then, was to get the guards shifted from that spot which was too close to the path he and Tinker would have to follow in order to reach the window.

He gave the lad a warning touch to stand steady, and bending down, felt about until his fingers encountered one of the edging stones of the path. It was a flattish bit of granite oval in shape and about six inches long by three wide, making a very convenient missile for what he had in mind. Gripping this as he would a ball, he brought his arm back and sent the stone skimming over the tops of the crotons to fall with a crash in some bushes a score of feet away.

The noise brought the sound of voices to an instant stop. There was silence for a little, then a voice sounded again, and Blake and Tinker clearly heard one of the guards say:

"Caramba! What was that?"

"Go and see," came another voice, "it is on your beat."

"By all the saints, but it is on yours— you have the centre—it fell straight out from here."

They might have continued to argue the point had Blake not sent another stone after the first. This time he put more strength into the heave, with the result that it crashed still farther away, and, as luck would have it, plunged full into a glass frame of some sort. At the sound of the splintering glass the three guards broke into excited questions, and then one of them plucked up courage enough to start and investigate.

His taunts decided his companions to follow him, and, just for good measure, Blake threw a third stone. When the sounds showed that the guards were poking about in the bushes, calling to whoever was there to come out, Blake caught Tinker by the sleeve, and stole round the bush which had sheltered them.

They streaked across the gravelled path like two shadows, and then along beside the building until they reached the little well. Blake was over the protecting railings and down to the bottom in a single leap, landing without a sound on his bare feet. Tinker thudded softly beside him, and, together, they set to work at the lower sash of the window.

Their guess was a good one. It rose easily after they once got it started, proof that the watchman inside had not bothered to make an examination since coming on duty. Once inside they closed it after them, and after peering out for a few moments to see if there were any signs of the guards Tinker, who had studied the arrangement of the room during the day, now took the lead. He stole across between piles of books and old bits of broken furniture until he reached the door. Here he paused, and together they once more listened.

Not a sound broke the silence of the great building. Once more the lad started on, passing the closed doors of the other store-rooms

—although they could not see that, so dark was it and feeling his way along until he had counted some thirty-odd paces. Then he gripped Blake's arm and began shuffling forward slowly, exploring ahead with his toe after each advance in order to find the bottom step. When he stubbed against it he gave Blake's arm a pressure, and then, side by side, they began to creep up.

The stairs were wide and winding. After every three or four they would pause to listen, but it was not until they had felt the door at the top that they heard any sound. It was of a nature that caused them to sink back, each flattening himself against the nearest wall. The sound that reached them was a steady padding that they guessed was the watchman on his rounds. As far as they could judge he seemed to be somewhere on the main floor, but it was not for some minutes that they caught the gleam of his lantern.

He was coming along the wide corridor into which the staircase debouched, and, if he continued, must pass close to them. If they remained where they were, and he glanced in that direction, he could not help but see them.

Blake saw this danger at once, and, reaching across in the darkness, pressed Tinker back a couple of steps. He himself remained where he was watching each shuffle that brought the watchman nearer. A dozen feet lay between them—two more paces brought the man still closer—a couple of yards, and then something streaked out from the gloom of the staircase, and before the watchman knew whence the attack had come a pair of powerful hands were at his throat choking off the startled cry that rose in his throat!

CHAPTER 5. Blake and Tinker Crack a Safe with Considerable Success.

SCARCELY had Blake's hands closed about the watchman's throat than Tinker was beside him just in time to catch the lantern before it struck the floor. Sliding it to one side, he grabbed the struggling watchman by the legs and, between them, they soon had him helpless. While Blake held him Tinker took the lantern and sped down to the basement. He left the light near the open door of the lumber-room through which they had passed and made for one corner where, earlier in the day, he had noticed a heap of rope bits. He chose some of these and sped back to the upper floor.

With the rope and a couple of course bandanas they bound and gagged their victim, after which they dragged him into a small room close by. That done, Blake took up the lantern, and, knowing the level of the windows in the front of the building were above the eye level of anyone outside, he boldly led the way through the main staff room and along a secondary corridor to a door at the far end.

This door opened into a small ante-room from which they gained a room beyond— the private bureau of the president of the republic, which was their objective that night. This apartment was a lofty, well furnished room which automatically became the bureau of each president as he was elected; but it was more of a formal meeting-place for him to discuss matters with the minister of the treasury than anything else, for it was rarely used. Off it was a larger room for the use of the minister of the treasury.

Don Cristofo Gouffra, the president, however, made considerably more use of the private room at the treasury than had most of his predecessors. In the short time he had been there, Sexton Blake had noticed that scarcely a day passed that the president did not appear, and by dint of careful inquiries added to his own observation he had come to the conclusion that Don Cristofo carried on the greater bulk of his private affairs in that apartment. There were many reasons why, for such a purpose, it would be much better than the rooms at the palace. And since Blake was firmly convinced that Don Cristofo was a rascal of the first water he had a strong desire to examine the contents of the big safe in the private bureau.

In fact, Blake had been in San Jose long enough to discover that every man-jack in the government was a rascally grafter with the

29

exception of one person. That lone exception was Don Fernando Alvarez, at whose secret behest Blake was there, so, that being so, whatever discoveries he might make could not rebound to the discredit of his client.

One thing that had convinced Blake of the extreme privacy of the matters dealt with by the president in that room was the size and newness of the safe.

On the few occasions when he had been able to get a glimpse of the interior of the apartment, his eyes had rested on this great strong box, and he had noticed that it was no antiquated affair such as one found in the other rooms of the treasury.

Instead, it was one of the latest models turned out by a certain big English firm, and the combination was of the American circular type, controlled by a series of turns and numbers.

It was not an easy safe to crack, but, on the other hand, Sexton Blake knew the science of lock construction as he knew the palm of his hand. It was one of the details of his profession which needed ceaseless study, and, had he wished to do so, he could have cut out a decidedly successful career for himself as a master cracksman.

The window of this room looked out on the northern end of the building, and, realising that a light would cause comment among the guards if it remained there for many minutes, Blake signed to Tinker to put a rug over the lantern in such a way that the beams were enclosed in a sort of funnel from which they could only shine on the door of the safe. Then he knelt down, and, while Tinker kept watch, Blake began to test the knob of the nickelled combination.

The type was one with which he was familiar enough; but that did not mean it was going to yield readily to his touch. On the contrary. There are many thousands of variations of numbers and turns which one may employ in this sort of combination, and in that lies their great advantage over the old-style ordinary key or letter combination safe.

It was all depending on which particular numbers and turns would cause the complicated arrangement of tumblers to fall, and each fall by no means meant that the secret was Blake's. He had to find the complete circuit, so to speak, before the bolts would slide back.

Had he been working under conditions where he could have brought his own equipment with him, he would have attached a small microphone to the door close to the dial in order to magnify the sound of the tumblers. But lacking this, he had to depend on his own sharp hearing, and when he had given the knob a preliminary whirl or two, he pressed one ear close to the steel, lowering his eyes so that he could watch the lines and figures on the dial.

He began with a turn to the right, a single twisting that he continued steadily, but with infinite "drag," waiting a moment each time the arrow cut on the knob was opposite one of the lines on the dial. These were marked with numbers at intervals of every five, and when he came to one of these he waited even longer. Round and round went the knob until it had made a complete circuit of the dial, and still not a single tell-tale sound had come from within.

A second time he made the turning, with the same result. A third time was equally barren, but when he had completed a fourth turning he heard the tell-tale click of the tumblers at the moment when the arrow mark pointed to number 65.

Unless his ears had betrayed him, that was a definite starting point. Now, according to the usual system employed, the next release number should be found in an opposite turning, and since the first number was found by a quadruple circuit, the next should be found in a triple turning to the left.

If that test failed, then he would know that a more complicated system was employed, and would have to seek for it. But he knew that the alternate plan was almost invariably adopted when the combinations were set before the safes were sent from the factory, and only a more unusual method used by special request of the purchaser.

Therefore he reversed the knob, and once more kept turning slowly and patiently, listening for a second tell-tale click of the tumblers. He hardly expected it the first or second time round, but in the third turning he went even more slowly, and it was when the indicating arrow was pointing to a line just two divisions from the longer one marked 50 that he heard what he was listening for. That would make the second number of the code, 48.

So far, so good. The system appeared, so far, to be the regular one, and, that being so, he should now reverse to the right again for a double circuit in order to get the third code number. He did so, and found he was right, for he had just about completed a second full circuit when he heard a clicking of the tumblers as the arrow was opposite 85. Excellent! He now had three of the code numbers; and, according to what he knew of the type, a fourth should complete the circuit.

He turned once more, a single turning to the left, and when the indicating line was at the number 35 the last and vital tell-tale fall of the tumblers sounded. Unless he was badly astray he should now be able to press back the handle which controlled the bolts. He raised his head to do so, memorising the combination code at the same time— four turns to the right, pause at number 65; three turns to the left, pause at number 48; two turns to the right, pause at number 85; one turn to the left, stop at number 55; then turn back the handle.

He did so, and a faint smile might have been seen on his lips as the handle went back easily, taking the three heavy bolts with it. The safe was at his mercy. He found, on swinging upon the heavy steel outer door, that he had still to get past an inner door of wood, but he had with him a small bunch of keys which never left him, and under his expert handling he soon had the second barrier open.

At first there seemed to be very little inside, the safe was divided into several vertical compartments in the lower half which had been intended for accounting books. There was only one book to be seen, and Blake ignored it. The upper half of the interior was given over to smaller horizontal divisions for papers and so on, with, in the centre, a small closed compartment having a door with knob for opening, but no lock.

Blake opened the little door, and found, as he had expected, that there were further small divisions inside, with two small locked drawers underneath. He had a hunch that it was in one of those drawers he would find what he was seeking, so once more he brought his keys into play.

He attacked the top drawer first. It proved a more difficult lock than that which had secured the first wooden door, but by dint of much patient twisting with his own little invention known as the "spider," he got it open.

Inside he saw first a heap of paper money, and a closer scrutiny showed him the notes were American "greenbacks," the bundle was held by a broad rubber band, and with a sign to Tinker he tossed it to the lad for counting.

Next he came upon a packet of papers. Slipping off the enclosing band, he gave them the "once-over." They proved to be share certificates in English and American companies—all good, solid issues, as Blake took note. He placed these on one side, and went through a bundle of other papers. These related to private property belonging to the president, to judge from the name in each, and held only an academic interest for Blake. Then there were some letters which he read unblushingly. One of these he abstracted, and placed inside his shirt; the others he returned to their envelopes, and laid them aside.

And that was all this little drawer yielded. What he had hoped to find was not there. In fact, he did not know that what he was looking for existed at all, but Blake was going on the theory that Don Cristofo Gouffra was playing a big game of graft with the resources of Santa Marta, and he knew that it would be almost impossible for him to be mixed up in the multitudinous details of a dozen or more schemes without having some private record. Indeed, the contents he had come upon so far seemed to strengthen that likelihood.

Before attacking the second drawer and, so far as he could tell, his last possibility of finding what he sought in this room, he glanced towards Tinker who had finished counting the money. His lifted eyebrows were a question. Tinker bent closer.

"Fifty thousand dollars, mostly in thousands," he whispered.

Blake nodded, and taking the bundle tossed it back in the drawer. He had his own ideas as to why Don Christofo kept such a large sum of foreign money in that safe. He replaced the other papers exactly as he had found them, then closed and locked the drawer.

Now he tackled the other, and after some more tricky work with the "spider" managed to force it open. And, as his eyes took in just one item in the drawer they narrowed with greater interest in the private safe of the president. He took out the object and held it so Tinker could see what it was. The lad made out that it seemed to be a thick morocco bound volume of the diary sort and, when Blake had scanned an item here and there, Tinker knew from the way he nodded his head that he had struck oil.

Quite coolly the detective dropped it inside his shirt with the letter he had purloined, and now lost no time in relocking the drawer. Followed the closing and securing of the larger wooden door, and after that the swinging to of the great steel slab. A pressure of the handle and a twirl of the knob was all that was needed to leave it just as it had been.

Their objective had been attained, but they had still to consolidate their position so to say, by beating a safe retreat—a matter that bristled with difficulties as they were soon to discover.

CHAPTER 6.   Blake and Tinker Stir Up a Hornets' Nest.

BEFORE attempting the getaway Blake drew the rug completely over the lantern and motioned Tinker towards one of the big windows that looked out on the northern part of the gardens. Tinker crept across and, raising himself, crouched close to the wide sill. Several minutes passed in silence; then he came creeping back to Blake.

"The guards are on the job," he whispered. "Two of them seem to be coming round each end and meeting just between the two windows of this room."

Blake nodded thoughtfully.

"That means we gave them a shaking up coming in," he whispered back. "That little ruse has cut both ways. I had thought of trying to leave by one of these windows, but I think we had better go the way we came. Let's have a shot at it, anyway."

With that he drew aside the rug and slid it back where it had lain. Then they crept out of the room to the ante-room, and from there into the secondary corridor. On reaching the main passage which ran right across the building Blake paused by the door of the cupboard where they had left the watchman.

"I think," he said in a low tone, "it will be as well to pull this fellow out a little—enough for his legs to obtrude. He won't be found until morning unless we are seen outside; but in any event there is no need for him to lie there longer than necessary."

Tinker opened the door and catching the prone figure by the feet dragged him out until most of his legs were in the corridor. Blake gave a nod that this would suffice, and then the two made their way along to the head of the stairs. Before descending Blake blew out the light, leaving the lantern on the floor at the head of the stairs. He was not particular that there should be any great mystery about the place having been visited during the night.

The bound watchman would have his own story to tell, and there was nothing to be gained by trying to make a greater mystery of it. They had secured the one thing they had come for, and no matter what the watchman might have to say it rested entirely with the president himself whether the truth were made public or not.

Once again Tinker took the lead. They descended the stairs without incident and reached the store-room through which they had entered. Standing under the window there they could hear, now and then, the steps of a guard passing. It was plain that the stirring up Blake had given them in coming was still having its effect. This meant that their means of retreat was practically closed, and they could not again employ the same strategy.

Blake bent close to the lad.

"I don't see anything for it but to get out and lie doggo in the area beneath the window," he breathed. "We might be able to make a dash between passings of the guard. The chances are about a hundred to one on that we shall be seen, and if we are they are liable to shoot first and ask questions after. They are nervy now, and anything unusual will make them jump. But we can't stay here all night. It isn't far from midnight. When the guard changes everyone will be more on the alert than usual, for an officer will be here. If we do have to make an open dash for it I think we had better settle now that we shall separate, each finding his own way back to the hut as best he can. Do you understand?"

"Yes, guv'nor. Do you mean that we will make a jump for it as soon as we are outside the window?"

"You will go first. Easy now—there goes the guard. Now he is past. Up with this window and out with you."

They slid the lower sash up a little and Tinker squirmed out, sinking immediately into the black shadow in the well. Blake followed, pulling the window down before dropping beside the lad. They crouched there until they once more heard the crunch of the guard's footsteps and flattened themselves back still more as the fellow passed not three feet above their heads. Blake gave him a few moments to get farther towards the end of the building; then he gripped Tinker by the shoulder.

"Up with you," he whispered urgently. "Over the rail and make for the back wall. Pay no attention to anything but making your getaway. Now!"

With that he literally heaved the lad over the railing, saw him drop lightly to the other side and disappear. Blake had his hands on the iron spikes ready to follow when, from close at hand, he heard a sharp exclamation followed by a harsh command.

"Halt!"

The lad had been seen.

Before Blake could move either way a shot rang out, and then a great confusion rose as the two end guards came rushing back towards the centre man who had seen Tinker streaking across the path. A second shot followed, a medly of excited voices asking futile questions, and then in the midst of it Blake swung himself over the railing.

He landed not twenty feet away from the trio, and as one of them spotted him he gaped and pointed. The other two swung sharply and the next instant one of the rifles crashed out again. A bullet zipped past Blake, crashing into the stone immediately behind him.

Blake had his pistol out by now, and as the three guards rushed him he tightened his finger on the trigger, he sent three shots from the heavy weapon into the ground at their feet. The sand kicked up in their faces, was sufficient to give them pause, and while they hesitated Blake was across the path like a flash and into cover of the bushes.

At his disappearance the guards broke into action, and at that moment the three who had been in the front came running round to see what was up. Blake paused for a moment to get his bearings, heard a terrific crashing in several different directions, wondered which would be Tinker, and then felt a great weight crash upon him. One of the guards, at least, was not lacking in physical courage.

It was sheer accident that the man had located Blake. In rushing blindly through the bushes he had stumbled full into him, and the next moment the two were on the ground fighting like a couple of ocelots. Blake knew his only hope was to make short work of this single antagonist. If the fellow was able to cling on to him until his comrades arrived they would overpower the detective by weight and bulk if in no other way.

Therefore Blake concentrated on getting the human fury stilled for a moment. Either sheer fright or exceptional courage was driving him to an activity that was amazing. His legs were working up and down while his arms were clawing upwards as if his life depended on getting a grip on Blake's throat.

Blake allowed him to get uppermost for one brief moment. There was no other way in which he could get him clear of the ground in order to make his own hold. But as soon as the other was astride him and was in the very act of opening his mouth to yell for his companions Blake struck.

Up came his knees, arms and body in one terrific heave. The man astride him shot off as if he had been catapulted, and so swiftly did Blake follow up his advantage that he had his man down flat on his back before he grasped what was happening.

Close beside him Blake felt the automatic which had fallen in the first rush. Snatching this up he reversed it and brought the butt down with a sharp tap between the other's eyes. It was not a "killing" tap, that, but it had enough behind it to put his man hors de combat for some minutes to come. As he slumped back Blake sprang to his feet and, pausing a moment to get his bearings again, continued his dash through the garden.

Somewhat to his surprise he was not molested. He reached the rear fence in safety and swung over to the road at the back. He looked up and down it for some signs of the lad but could see no one.

Thinking that Tinker had already succeeded in getting clear and was probably by now streaking it for the adobe hut at top speed Blake broke into a jog-trot which he kept up until he turned into the plaza. Then he slowed down to the shuffle of the country making across the plaza in a diagonal direction, never dreaming that at that very moment Tinker was having a very warm time of it back in the garden.

On first clearing the railing when Blake had heaved him over, Tinker had raced across the path as Blake had seen. His dash had been the cause of all the rumpus that followed, but even then he would have got clear quite all right had it not been that the first shot caused him to swerve.

He found himself almost at once in a tangle of black palm than which there is nothing more difficult from which to extricate oneself. Very precious moments were lost here, and by the time he was clear of the thorns the pack was upon him.

It was the row which Tinker was making that most of the guards mistook for the passage of the second person who had dashed from the shadow beneath the window. It was this that explained why Blake had only one pursuer to contend with when he figured Tinker ought to be clear of the grounds. But at that moment the lad was in the thick of a desperate battle against ever-growing odds.

Two of the guards had found him, but those who had raced round from the front of the building had quickly joined in, and before Tinker could break away and make a run for it he was being mauled by five clawing fiends who, now that they thought the cause of their previous fright was only this apparently young native who had been prowling about, laid into him lustily to show what great fellows they were.

In the heat of the battle they felt but did not pause to wonder at the distinctly gringo type of blows which the lad was employing. As a matter of fact Tinker gave them no pause to do so. Realising that he had stumbled into a bad mess he exerted every effort to break clear long enough to get his pistol into action. But they pressed him too closely, and it was only by deliberately allowing them to rush him back into the stinging embrace of the black palm bush that he gained a moment's breather.

Despite the agony of the stabbing thorns he fought his way clean through it, arriving on the other side with blood dripping from a score of wounds. His assailants who had not followed through had nipped round the shrubbery to meet him, but this time there was no withstanding the charge which drove through them.

The pain of the thorn pricks had put Tinker into a very bad temper, and it was the steam engendered by this rage that, for the time being, made him irresistible.

He plunged on blindly, drove head-first into a tree, and as he staggered back half stunned felt the pack upon him again. Somehow he managed to get his automatic out, but before he could use the business end of it he was being pressed so close that all he could do was bring the butt smashing down.

He felt the heavy metal strike something and then the space immediately in front of him was clear. He stumbled over a prone body and struck a second time. Another of his assailants went down, and the rest held back at this new development.

It was just at this critical moment when the game was coming into the lad's hands that two other figures came plunging through the gloom. An authoritative voice demanded to know what was going on, and Tinker knew it for that of an officer. This could only mean that the midnight change was due, and, therefore, a full extra half-dozen guards must have arrived.

Tinker had no thought now of trying to vanquish the remainder. All he wanted was a clear run of a few yards and he had no doubt about getting away. But with a thick bush behind him and that human wall in front of him it was not easy. The only way was through those who hemmed him in, and before the officer could repeat his question Tinker had started.

He lowered his head, held the reversed automatic ready in his hand and plunged forward. The sheer force of his weight and determination carried him clean through the three who were immediately in front of him; but as he cleared them he felt the weight of a body crash upon him. It was the officer who was game enough, and it did not take Tinker long to discover that this wiry young man knew something about rough and tumble fighting.

He dropped his weapon and tried to get a grip on the other's wrists. The officer had landed on his back, and as Tinker reached back he jammed one knee into the small of the lad's back, rendering him helpless for one precious moment. The pain of the pressure against the spine caused Tinker to go limp, and while he staggered from side to side the other got a half nelson grip that he had never learned in Santa Marta. As a matter of fact that particular young officer had spent a couple of years in Europe where he had picked up more than French and British ideas of military training. He had learned a little fighting at the same time.

Any other officer in the whole Santa Marian army would not have mattered greatly. Tinker had been so nearly through that it would have been impossible to hold him. It was sheer bad luck that this particular young fellow should have been the one on guard duty that night for, once he had Tinker momentarily helpless, he lost no time in clinching his advantage.

Back and back and back he dragged the lad until Tinker felt that his spine must snap. The pain from thighs to shoulder blades was atrocious; but still he struggled against it until one terrific heave snapped his resistance. It was a case of give in or go down with a broken spine and the lad was human.

In one last effort he allowed his muscles to relax. As the other followed him, intending to administer the coup de grace, Tinker plunged upwards in a sudden effort that carried him clear. With a desperate break he rolled to one side and was almost on to his hands and knees when something swished through the gloom and hit him on the back of the head. A million constellations danced across a firmament which seemed to stretch into an eternity of cosmic chaos; then he hurtled into a pit of utter night.

One of the guards had stunned him with the butt-end of a rifle!

40

CHAPTER 7.   San Jose is Treated to a Sensation—Sexton Blake Pulls Some Strings.

BY two hours after midnight Blake knew definitely that a serious hitch had occurred.

There had been time and to spare for Tinker to return even if he had found it necessary to make a complete detour of the whole town. Then, in some way, disaster had overtaken him. But how? That was what was puzzling Blake as he sat in the darkness just within the open door of the adobe hut, peering up and down the mean street for some sign of the lad.

Blake had felt certain that the lad was well away before him. In that case what could he have met to detain him? Once he himself had got clear of the grounds the way had been clear. Thinking things over he was a little puzzled now that he had not been more hotly pursued and he began to wonder if, after all, Tinker had not gained the wall as he had thought.

If not then it might well be that he had run into the arms of the guards. In that case something must be done at once. If the lad's identity were discovered or, even if it were found that he was not a native it would complicate matters seriously. All the quiet work which they had put in during that week in the capital would be wasted and their usefulness ended for this matter at least. He must make sure without delay.

He started out once more, making his way in roundabout fashion in the direction of Cristobal Plaza. There he slowed down to an idling pace and walked along past the front of the treasury. At first sight everything appeared perfectly normal. He could see the guards at the front, walking up and down, and there wasn't a light showing to indicate that anything unusual was going on inside.

But Blake could not get rid of the uneasy feeling that Tinker had been caught. If so, had he been dragged off somewhere? Or was he incarcerated somewhere in the treasury building? At any risk, he must find out what had taken place.

Continuing on to the very end of the gardens he turned down a narrow, dusty lane to the right, and in this way gained the back of the gardens from which he had fled not so long before. He kept in close against the wall as he moved along, and when he came once more to the shadow of the tree that had already served him well he paused to peer up and down the road.

He could see no one moving, so with a light leap he gained the top of the wall. It was an easy matter to swing himself down on to the soft turf and now, knowing more of the lay-out of the gardens than before, he was able to steal along silently until he was once more close to the path that ran at the back of the building, he sank deep into the shadow of some bushes there and lay listening.

He could hear the pacing of the three guards as they passed up and down, up and down, and for a matter of a quarter of an hour or so, during which his patience was sorely tried, he heard absolutely nothing else. He was wondering why there was this strict attention to duty. He knew the guard had been changed and that the soldiers now on sentry-go would be fresher than those who had been relieved.

But, even so, it was not like the Santa Martan soldier to miss a chance of gossip. Blake knew nothing of the stern shaking up the guards had received from the young officer who had come on the scene at the time of Tinker's capture.

Then came a pause in the pacing and the low murmur of voices reached him. Followed the scraping of a match and a tiny flare of light as one of them lit a cigarette. Blake moved so he could see the faint glow of the tobacco as the man inhaled, and then he grew still more alert as he heard one say to the other:

"The senor captain will be round again, think you?"

"No, hombre, not to-night. He is too pleased with his capture. He will remain at the cuartel to report to the officer of the day."

"Quien sabe. He may have been prowling about to see what he could pick up. There is talk, hombre, of plotting on the coast. One never knows. He may have been a spy. But we have nothing to worry over. We were not on duty."

"True. But someone was inside the building. The watchman says that he was attacked by a round dozen savage fellows all of whom were armed to the teeth and threatened to slit his heart out if he so much as whispered."

Blake could not help smiling at the words. It was evident that the watchman had garnished up the facts considerably in order to explain why he permitted himself to be overpowered.

The two sentries began talking again, but Blake had heard enough. He knew now that Tinker had been captured—mestizo, it appeared, they thought him. And investigations must have been made inside the building for, it seemed, the watchman had been found. There had been no mention of the safe in the president's room, so Blake took it that, so far, nothing was known about this. And Tinker had been taken to the cuartel, which is the equivalent of gaol.

That was the most important item he had heard. He had no further interest here; he had to do something quickly about Tinker. If what he had just overheard was true then Tinker would be examined within a few hours by the officer of the day. These guards did not seem to suspect that he was a European, but a close examination would soon reveal the truth. This must be prevented at any cost. But how?

Blake began to creep back the way he had come. Foot by foot and yard by yard he retreated until the murmur of the guards' voices died away. Then he risked getting to his feet, and in a few minutes was once more under the friendly tree. A swing up, a pause on the wall, then he landed lightly in the dust on the other side.

He hurried along in the shadow until he gained the plaza. From there he went by the shortest route he knew to the little adobe hut. Once inside, he closed the door and lighted a candle. Then, seating himself at the plain wood table, he puffed thoughtfully at a cigarette, trying to solve the problem which confronted him.

It had already been stated why Blake was in San Jose. Don Fernando Alvarez, the Minister of Finance, had sent for him secretly for, as has been hinted, Don Fernando was the only honest member of a government that was corrupt with graft from the president, Don Christofo Gouffra, to the lowliest clerk in the service. For three or four years the credit of the little republic had been declining steady. It had come as no surprise to those who knew what was going on when the Santa Martan government had repudiated the interest on its bonds. No government could provide a picking for everyone in it and meet its proper debts.

Don Fernando was looked upon as being a crook and grafter just like every other member of the government. But this was an injustice. For a long time he had been striving to uncover sufficient proof to make a public statement of conditions. He was prepared to come out into the open and risk his own name and career in order to do so, for Don Fernando loved his country, such as it was, and was a true patriot. Nor did he need stolen wealth, for he was a large owner of cattle, and coffee estates and very rich in his own right.

But try as he would he had been unable to put his finger on anything more than a few unimportant peccadiloos of junior clerks. This would not suffice. What he was after was proof against no less a person than the president himself—proof that would be so undeniable, an impeachment must follow. But the rogues about him were too clever. Their tracks were kept too well covered. Yet he knew that somewhere among the books in the treasury he could find this proof if he only knew how to search for it.

This deadlock lasted for some months. Then, one day, Don Fernando, who was a close student of the European press, happened to read in a certain London newspaper of a recent case which Sexton Blake, the famous criminologist, had brought to a spectacular finish. The case had to do with certain insurance scandals, and when he read the evidence Don Fernando realised that this man, Sexton Blake, had an almost uncanny grasp of finance and figures. The idea was born in his mind that if he could but get hold of a man like Blake to undertake the search for evidence it would be found.

Again and again the thought had recurred to him and each time he had brushed it aside. A man so busy in Europe could not be persuaded to come away out to Santa Marta on a job that might take weeks, or even months of his time. Don Fernando had read in the paper the amount of the fee Blake had received for unveiling the insurance scandals and by that he could gauge how Blake stood in his profession.

But he could not get the idea out of his mind and, at last, when things began to get worse and worse and a new loan was mooted (out of which back interest on other loans was to be paid while the rest of the money went into the pockets of the grafters) Don Fernando could stand it no longer.

As minister of the treasury he would have to sign these new bonds, although the negotiations would be carried out entirely by the president. And Don Fernando could not bring himself to be a party to this new colossal fraud. Then, too, he knew there was a strong element of dissatisfied anti-government forces down on the coast where the money and power really lay, and he feared that the talk of a new loan would precipitate a revolution.

He had heard whispers of General Primo de Miguel being back in the country, and he knew that wily old soldier well enough to realise that if he knew a new loan was to be a fact he would leave no stone unturned to put himself in the presidential chair before the money reached Santa Marta, so that he and his accomplices could have the pickings. The alternative was a new government under Don Fernando, but that upright statesman was not prepared to put himself forward until he could rally the best elements about him in the face of actual proof of Don Cristofo's duplicity.

Don Fernando had a daughter—a delightful, beautiful girl who had not long been back from Europe where she had been at school in Paris and London. To her the minister was sent to confide all his secrets and it was due to her that he finally wrote a confidential letter to Sexton Blake. To his surprise—but not to that of Senorita Carlotta—Blake had replied in encouraging terms, and the upshot was that when Don Fernando had replied giving concrete particulars, Sexton Blake had cabled that he would come out to San Jose and see what could be done.

Then Blake had devised the scheme of appearing in San Jose as an accountant from Bogota, and in this way he was able to gain access to the books without anything being suspected.

The clerks who had doctored the books were quite confident that no so-called accountant from Bogota would be clever enough to uncover the true state of affairs. If they had known that the eagle eye of the most famous criminologist living was poring over those pages, they would have experienced very different feelings.

Nor did it take long for Blake to come to the conclusion that Don Fernando was right. The accounts reeked with subterfuge. There was scarcely a page where payments had not been faked. The contract books revealed an appalling state of affairs. There were dozens of contracts given out to persons who had received large advances from the government, and yet, so far as Blake could discover, had not performed a peso's worth of work against them.

There were huge allocations to various committees that had never sat. There were thousands of pesos paid over with disturbing regularity to the president's entertaining account—an account that could not very well be analysed, for the head of the state could not be asked for a detailed account of expenditure.

Everything was rotten the whole way through, and before he had been at the treasury three days, Blake had proof and to spare that Don Cristofo was "milking" the country at a rate that would have made some of the captains of industry of Wall Street lick their lips in envy.

That was when Blake came to the conclusion that the only way to plunge to the very heart of the whole scandal was to "get the goods" on Don Cristofo, so to say.

This suggestion he had put up to Don Fernando at a secret meeting. Senorita Carlotta, who had been present, and, incidentally, had been making Tinker considerably unsettled from the battery of her dark, lovely eyes, had endorsed Blake's suggestion fervently. She hated Don Cristofo for personal reasons, for the president had a son—a simpering, greasy, conceited little rat, who had offered again and again for Carlotta's hand. And Carlotta would have none of him.

Don Cristofo had used his official position to harass both Carlotta and her father in the matter, and while Don Fernando had been suavely tactful, Carlotta, whose ideas had been broadened in England, had refused the suitor in no unmeasured terms. Therefore, she jumped at the chance to see Don Cristofo come a cropper.

Don Fernando would not say "yes" or "no." But he agreed to do all he could to make this possible for Blake, and it was finally decided that Blake should take his own lead in the matter. The result was that, when he was satisfied Don Cristofo must have hidden records which would condemn him, Blake had watched constantly to discover something that would give him a clue.

Now it has already been explained that each president of Santa Marta automatically became entitled to a private room at the treasury. This room had been seldom used in the past, but both Blake and Tinker noticed that Don Cristofo was in the habit of coming there frequently. In that room he gave many interviews, and it did not take Blake long to discover that almost invariably those interviews were followed by further payments from the treasury.

Still Blake and Tinker kept watch, and the big safe in the private room finally intrigued Blake to such an extent that he could not rest until he had seen the interior and what it contained. He had figured that this safe would be an excellent strong box for secrets if Don Cristofo had any to conceal.

Hence the expedition that night. And now Blake was facing the problem of Tinker's capture. How to effect the lad's release before he could be interrogated by the officer of the day? Somehow, in some way, Don Fernando's influence would have to be brought to bear. But how? Back and forth Blake's mind mulled over the matter. If Don Fernando should be out at his hacienda, some twenty miles from the city, then his aid was out of the question. And even if he were at his official town residence, how could he pull the strings?

Don Fernando was nervous of moving too fast. That Blake knew. And with Tinker's capture threatening exposure of the whole plot, he might get panicky and pull in his horns entirely. Yet he must be brought to exert his influence before morning. If not—

And at that moment a new idea came to Blake. It was the thought of Senorita Carlotta. She would be greatly distressed to hear what had happened, and, unless he had misjudged her completely, Blake had an idea she would be only too ready to lend her aid to the rescue of Tinker if she knew what to do.

Should he apply direct to her and leave it to her Spanish penchant for intrigue to get the lad out of his scrape? The more he thought of it the more Blake liked the idea. He would try it, at any rate. If she was at the hacienda, then it would, of course, misfire.

Taking a piece of very cheap writing paper and a pointed nib, such as the average Santa Martan would use, Blake dipped the tip into a pot of purple ink and set to work to compose a letter to Carlotta. When he was satisfied with it, this was what he had evolved:

"Senorita.

"Complications have arisen in which I need your assistance most urgently. What has to be done must be done before morning. Therefore, I am taking this to your house in the hope that you will be there and not at the hacienda. I shall do my best to get a servant to give it to your duenna to take to you. If it reaches you I shall be waiting. On the solution of this rests the fate of everything.

"I am your humble and respectful servant,
"RAMON CASTRO."

Blake thought it wiser, in case the letter should be read by eyes other than those for which it was intended, he should use the name by which he was known in San Jose. If this should happen, then it might be regarded as nothing more than some love intrigue in which the senorita was amusing herself.

But he did not go to the house as Ramon Castro. That, he knew, would be fatal. Instead, he kept to the disguise of a poor peon which he still wore, and with the letter tucked inside his shirt, started out to deliver it in person—he to pose as a messenger from someone else.

Don Fernando's official residence was not far from Cristobal

Plaza. On his way there Blake took occasion to pass again in front of the treasury building, but everything seemed quite normal.

On reaching his destination, he found, as he had expected, the great outer doors closed, but he knew the custom of the country and knew a peon should be sleeping on guard just inside. So he kept up a gentle tap-tap-tap-tap on the blackwood panel until, at last, he heard someone stirring within. Still he persisted in his summons, and then there came the rattle of bolts and a chain. The great door swung inwards a few inches, and he espied a face in the gloom.

"Que quere?" demanded the peon inside.

Blake took out the envelope and pushed it at him.

"Not so loud, hombre," he whispered. "I have brought a letter for the senorita who lives here. It must reach her without delay!"

"A letter for the senorita! The senorita Alvarez knows no one who sends letters at such an hour as this."

And with that the peon made to close the door. But Blake got his shoulder in the aperture.

"Fool!" he hissed. "This is no ordinary matter. It is a letter for which the senorita waits." He knew if Senorita Carlotta had been at the hacienda the man would have said so at first. "If you do not wake her duenna and see that she gets it now—NOW, you understand—it will be the worse for you. And here, my patron has been generous. I will share with you."

At that, Blake slipped a gold colone piece into the other's hand, and this worked the oracle.

"Wait here, then," he grumbled. "I will see. But if it gets me into trouble you will have to pay me more than this."

"All right; but make haste."

The peon would not permit him to come inside, so he had to cool his heels in the street, while the other shuffled off on his errand. The time passed slowly, and at every sound he heard Blake flattened himself in the shadow, for he did not want to be discovered there by any passing police. However, no one came until the peon once more opened the door, and this time he dropped the chain entirely.

"Come," he commanded, "but see that you make no noise. The senorita will come to you presently."

He closed and bolted the door, then he led Blake through the great patio to a small scented arbour in the far corner. There he left him, charging him to be silent until his mistress should come to him.

Just near the arbour Blake could make out the shadowy line of a balustrade. This, he figured, would be a staircase to the family quarters above, and soon after he saw he was right, for it was down these stairs that a wraith-like figure stole.

It was Carlotta, and as she peered through the gloom, seeing what she thought was only a strange peon, she drew back. But Blake whispered to her in English.

"It is all right, Senorita Alvarez—it is I."

"Oh!"

She breathed her relief and came to him with outstretched hands.

"What is it?" she asked anxiously. "What has happened?"

Blake told her briefly in whispers what had overtaken Tinker. She listened in silence; but when he had finished she gripped his arm tensely.

"We must do something at once. We cannot go to my father for he is out at the hacienda. But let me think, Mr. Blake, let me think."

She sank down on a bench, drawing Blake with her. Then the two sat there in the gloom of the tropic night while the girl's nimble mind canvassed the possibilities of the situation. Blake's mind was quiescent. He knew that, for the moment, he had done all he could. It was now up to Carlotta, and he had a hunch that she would think of something.

And he was right, for at last the girl turned to him, and, under the brilliant stars, he could see her dark eyes literally glowing with excitement. She laughed softly so close to his cheek that her warm breath was a light, scented caress.

CHAPTER 8.   Senorita Carlotta Takes a Hand.

"I'VE got it," she whispered. "Listen. Captain Gouffra, the president's son, was here this evening. He prattled as usual while I and my duenna were forced to listen. I paid little attention to what he said, but I am almost sure he mentioned that he was on the roster as officer of the day at the cuartel for this morning. He would not miss an opportunity to boast of that. If that is right, then there is a chance."

Blake knew that her mind was weaving some scheme of which the president's son was the intended victim, and the imprisoned Tinker the gainer. But he could not quite gather what she meant.

She laughed again when he asked her to explain.

"I will go to the cuartel," she said. "I already have a plan in my mind. I shall take my duenna and she will help me. Don't ask me any more now, Mr. Blake, but be patient. Before I come away from the cuartel Senor Tinker will be free—I, Carlotta Alvarez say it."

Blake heaved a sigh of relief. It was something of a novelty for him to find someone else doing the thinking and planning. Yet he had an extraordinary confidence in this soft and lissome girl who seemed as keen as mustard to pit her wits against Captain Gouffra, whom she hated like a corral snake.

"But if Captain Gouffra discovers that you are fooling him?" he asked.

"Poof! What does it matter? I care not for what he thinks. Caramba! He dare not say a word, Mr. Blake. I shall fool him and then I shall laugh at him, and to save his own face he will not dare tell the truth. He will blame someone else, and it will end there. You shall see that I am right."

Blake smiled and laid a firm brown hand on hers.

"I trust you to the hilt, senorita. I am prepared to leave it entirely in your hands. I don't know what I should do without you.

"You will find me eager to help at all times if it means that we shall bring down those who are ruining my poor country," she returned. "They must all—all fall, Mr. Blake; and Santa Marta must be purged."

And it was then Blake realised the girl was filled with a fine patriotism and love of country. She would stand the test, he knew now; she might bend but she would never break. She was an ally worth having.

50

They talked in whispers for some time longer; then she led Blake through the patio to the gate. As soon as the peon had let him out he started off leisurely in the direction of the Cristobal Plaza. He noticed that the first faint streaks of light were beginning to show in the east over the sierras. Dawn would not be long in coming now and Carlotta would have little time to put her plan into execution.

If she were mistaken about Captain Gouffra being on the roster as officer of the day, then it would all fall to the ground in any case. But Blake chose to believe that she was right; and he was filled with a lively anticipation as he crossed the square and made his way down a side street in the direction of the cuartel where Tinker was incarcerated.

Blake took up his position not far from the gates. There was nothing to cause comment in a peon lounging about at that hour of the morning. As a matter of fact, several person's were already abroad, making in the direction of the market where everything would soon be in full swing. And peons who took the trouble to get abroad early could usually pick up a casual job there. Hence no one cast a second look at the peon who sank down on his heels against a wall opposite the cuartel and lit a cigarette.

He was there when the officer of the day rode up. Dawn was a mass of gold over the sierras now, and, in the growing light, he had no difficulty in recognising Captain Gouffra. So Carlotta had not been mistaken. Just then the bell for early mass began to toll in the great belfry of the cathedral on the other side of the plaza, and soon many persons were abroad, most of them being women with black mantillas drawn over their heads. In this hurrying churchwards, Carlotta attracted no undue attention as she came along accompanied by her duenna.

Blake recognised her at once, even though the magnificent black lace mantilla was drawn about her face until only her eyes showed. Her duenna, a bulky figure in heavy black draperies, was between the girl and Blake, but her eyes were downcast and she did not see the roguish side-glance the lovely girl gave to the dirty-looking peon who sat against the wall. Then they passed into the cuartel and Blake sat waiting, wondering just how she was going to work the oracle.

He was told all about it later on, and when he knew the full story he regretted keenly that it had not been possible for him to be presont to witness how Carlotta wound the enamoured Captain Gouffra about her finger. For this is what happened.

The cuartel in San Jose was a combination of military and civil gaol. But it was entirely under army control, and conducted along military lines. Hence it was that, although there was a permanent gaoler in charge, there was too, an officer of the day whose duty it was to make a morning and evening inspection of all prisoners, as well as to interrogate any new ones brought in. This, then, is what Captain Gouffra had meant was to be his duty, when he told Senorita Carlotta that he would be officer on duty at the cuartel the following morning.

When Carlotta and her duenna entered, Captain Gouffra was seated at a table in a bare, white-washed room scanning the list of prisoners which the gaoler had produced for his inspection. At the bottom of this list were five names of prisoners brought in since the day before, and among those five names was that of one, "Juan Castro," which Tinker had given when forced to declare himself. Juan Castro was as good as any, and as common in Spanish America as John Smith or John Brown would have been in England.

The captain was on the point of having the five new prisoners summoned to his presence when, happening to glance past the gaoler who stood by the table, he saw, to his amazement, the two women on the point of entering. Then, as Carlotta drew aside her mantilla he recognised her. The greasy little fellow came to his feet with a jump, sending the chair over backwards and almost precipitating the gaoler after it in his eagerness to reach the girl.

"Senorita," he cried, "this is a wonderful and unexpected pleasure. To think that you would honour this dingy cell with your sweet presence."

Carlotta smiled at him in an alluring, provoking way which she had never used with him before. The captain was thrilled to his boots at this sign of graciousness and began to think that his fervent words of the previous evening had caused such an impression that she had found it impossible to proceed to early mass without first sneaking a word to him. And Carlotta let him think so. She was playing a game in which all was fair.

"I knew everything would be all right when I remembered that you were officer of the day," she murmured, giving him her hand. "I told the senora she must not worry, that you were too chivalrous to see her suffer."

The captain looked slightly bewildered. He hadn't the ghost of a notion what the girl was talking about. But he played lip.

"I am your slave, senorita—and," he added hastily, "the slave of the senora too."

Again her eyes smiled tenderly upon him and Captain Gouffra's head reeled. A little more of that and he would have been gibbering.

"Have you had him before you yet?" went on Carlotta. "I know you will be just and patient."

This was too much. He had to know what she was talking about.

"Forgive me, wonderful one," he began, but Carlotta cut in:

"How stupid of me, dear Captain Gouffra. I was forgetting. But how could you know. It is about a prisoner you have here. He was brought in last night. And the senora is very anxious. You see, he is but a lad and comes from a village beyond the pampas. He is, in a way, a relation of the senora's and she has just heard that he was playing some pranks in the garden of the treasury when he was set upon and arrested. I told her that as long as you were here it would be all right. So I have brought her to see him. You will let her go to him, won't you?" And when she pouted her lips like that Captain Gouffra would have thrown open the whole cuartel had she demanded it. Besides, the suspicion he was being played with never entered his head. He was far too conceited. He thought that the girl was secretly greatly impressed by his importance and wasn't it proof that she should come to him when she was in trouble? Of a certainty—yes—caramba! he would show her what a gallant officer he was.

"You say—a relative of the senora's," he said. "I know nothing about it. I have just come on duty. But I will find out. Be seated, I pray you."

"Thank you, but we will stand. The senora—"

Captain Gouffra turned to the gaoler.

"You have heard," he snapped, "Have you such a prisoner?"

"Si, senor captain, but—"

The gaoler had paused with a sidelong look at the women.

"But what? Speak out."

"He is young, it is true, but he is not thought to be harmless, senor. He was found in the treasury gardens. But it is believed that he had been inside. Several persons broke into the treasury building last night and overpowered the watchman. There is a report on the table, senor."

Captain Gouffra moved towards the table in order to read the report. This was the first he had heard of the business, and he was wondering what it could all be about. But Carlotta had no intention that he should read that report before she had made her stroke. So she called softly:

"Jaime."

At the sound of his Christian name the captain turned and his eyes grew heavily suffused as he looked at that maddening vision. He hesitated, then walked back, standing before her like a young cockerel, pluming himself and tugging at the misplaced eyebrow which he called a moustache.

"You called me," he said foolishly.

"Senora is not young—Jaime. Can't the report wait? You will not refuse to allow her to go to her young relative and have a few words with him. I—I shall remain here with you—Jaime."

That was enough. His blood was water and his senses a merry-go-round.

"Of course," he stuttored. "The senora shall go at once. And you, wonderful one, shall remain with me."

She still smiled at him while he snapped his fingers and gave the gaoler a command. Aside from the fact that the young man was officer of the day, he was also the son of the president, and if he had commanded the gaoler to throw open the door of every cell the man would have obeyed. He was one of the many units who plied a crooked graft, and therefore the word of a Gouffra was law.

He straightened his tunic and saluted; then he bowed to the duenna.

"If the senora will follow me," he said pompously.

The duenna, with bent head, turned to do so. Carlotta caught her by the hand and whispered to her, seemingly giving her words of comfort. Then the woman passed through the door and Carlotta turned her batteries once more on the young man.

In his cell Tinker sat on the edge of a bare plank wondering what was to be the upshot of this mess into which he had got himself. He had regained consciousness only after he had been brought to the cuartel and while he had given the name of "Juan Castro," he had obstinately remained silent when he was pressed to give an account of what he had been doing in the treasury gardens. He knew his only game just then was a waiting one, in order to give Blake some chance to make a move— if anything was possible.

Therefore he was considerably surprised to see an elderly woman, whose black garments told him she was a duenna, enter the cell. In the gloom he could not see her features plainly enough to recognise her as the duenna he had seen with Senorita Alvarez, and he thought a mistake must have occurred when the door slammed and the gaoler walked back along the corridor.

But the duenna knew her own countrymen only too well and, realising that the gaoler could easily come back without his bare feet making any noise on the stone floor, she played her part to the end. Rushing across the cell she threw herself upon the astonished Tinker, crying as she did so:

"Oh, my poor one! What will my poor sister say when she knows that her child is in this place? Oh, what have you done? What did you go to the treasury gardens for? Why have you fought with the good soldiers of the republic?"

Her heavy draperies were almost strangling Tinker and, thinking a mad woman had been thrust in upon him, he was struggling to get clear when he heard her whisper sharply in his ear:

"Act a part, senor—act a part."

Tinker then grasped something of the truth and in surly tones, he growled that he had only been walking through the gardens when he had been set upon for no reason. All the time the duenna was keeping up a heavy sobbing, and she continued this until there came a slight sound from the corridor. This time the gaoler had actually retreated.

She lost no time now. It went sorely against the grain for her to throw aside her usual frigid dignity to do this thing for gringoes, even if they were friends of the Alvarez family. But she would have done a lot when Carlotta wheedled her, the loyal soul.

Drawing away from Tinker, she crossed herself devoutly, no doubt asking forgiveness from her patron saint. Then she whispered:

"Turn your back, young senor. I have to take off these outer garments. I have worn two dresses. Be ready to get into one of them."

Tinker, who needed no further telling what was afoot, jumped up with alacrity and stood with his face to the wall. There followed some rustling sounds, then he heard her whisper:

"Now."

He turned to find a heap of black clothes lying on the floor, but to his eyes the woman looked as bulky as before. With deft fingers she got him into the sombre wraps, then she whispered her injunctions.

"When the gaoler opens the door you will pass out. Keep the mantilla over your face and your head down. Pretend to be sobbing if you can. Follow the gaoler until you come to the front. Senorita is waiting there, and will do the rest. I shall call now to the gaoler and then stand in the shadow until you are gone."

"But you, senora," protested Tinker. "Won't there be trouble? I don't want my freedom if you are to suffer."

Her eyes softened a little.

"I shall be all right. Senorita Carlotta will know what to do. Now be ready."

She went to the door and, after rattling the bars, called to the gaoler. When she heard him coming along she made a sign to Tinker and sped into one corner, where she would be out of sight of the man who opened the door. Tinker, trying his best not to appear clumsy in the draperies he had assumed, was standing just inside the door when the gaoler turned the key.

He had drawn the mantilla across his face and his head was bent as if in deep sorrow. Now and then he would give a convulsive heave of the shoulders, and it was in this fashion that he walked slowly along after the gaoler. The latter had given only a cursory glance into the cell. He had seen a dim figure in one corner, and had taken it for granted it must be his prisoner.

Through the side corridor into the main hall they went, and then as they neared the front floor, Tinker caught a glimpse of the inspection-room through an open door. He saw Senorita Alvarez facing him, but he did not turn in. He slowed down, causing his shoulders to heave harder than ever, and he was shuffling slowly towards the front door and freedom when there came a flurry of footsteps close to him, and a hand was laid on his arm. He jumped, for he thought his disguise had been penetrated. But it was only Carlotta, who was murmuring:

"My poor darling—my poor dear—come, let me take you home at once. This has been too much for you. You must not grieve so over the young wretch. The good Captain Gouffra assures me that his punishment will be only nominal. Come, my poor old nurse, and let Carlotta comfort you."

In this fashion they passed through the door and out on to the path, while Captain Couffra and the gaoler feigned a sympathetic bearing. As they reached the street and started along towards the plaza the heaving of Tinker's shoulders was perfectly genuine, for he was finding it difficult to keep from yelling aloud with joy at the way Gouffra had been fooled.

But they were not yet out of the wood, and when he spotted Blake lounging against the wall opposite the gaol, he knew that it would still be too risky to make a break for it.

So, with Carlotta continuing to pat his shoulder comfortingly and Blake idling along behind them, they reached the corner and turned into the plaza. The moment they did so Carlotta leant against the nearest wall and put one hand to her side. Her eyes were brimming with laughter, but she held herself in.

"Caramba, my poor duenna! You are so droll, Senor Tinker, I could not have kept it up much longer. But there is danger yet. You must get away at once. Here is the Senor Blake. He will now take care of you. I daren't remain and be seen talking to a peon. I shall see you both soon—Senor Blake has a plan."

With that she was gone, slowing up a little as she met Blake to whisper that it was really Tinker who was ahead, and who now had started on again, his head still down like some poor woman in deep distress. Blake knew he must not stop to speak, but as he nodded his head he whispered: "You are a perfect brick, senorita." And that blunt English compliment made the girl flush with a pleasure that all the flowery Spanish compliments ever invented would not have produced.

Blake continued on after Tinker until they were through the plaza. Then he overtook him, muttering as he passed:

"Follow the way I go and for the love of Mike shorten your steps; you are striding along like the gloomy Dane."

Tinker snorted, but shortened his pace, and in this fashion the pair kept right on out of the town until they came to some rough coulee stretches half a league out. There Blake turned into one of the deepest ravines and as soon as Tinker had joined them, they made short work of the disguise.

"Thanks, guv'nor. You and Senorita Carlotta make some team when you work together. What now?"

"We keep right, on moving—and, incidentally, you can give the whole of the credit to Carlotta. It was all her brain that did it. By now she has told young Gouffra how she tricked him, and he is quite equal to setting a whole company of cavalry on the trail. I don't think so though; I have an idea that resourceful young woman can handle him. But we can't take any chances. We must reach Don Fernando's hacienda before nightfall. If the president discovers to-day, as I think he will, what has happened to the contents of his safe there will be Hades popping. We've got to get under cover. Now come on."

With that they started on foot through the wild scrub country in a general direction that would bring them to the Alvarez hacienda before night. And just about then Carlotta was revealing to Captain Gouffra a few things that took the curl out of that young man's hair.

Carlotta had not returned directly to the gaol. She was anxious to secure the release of her duenna as quickly as possible, but she was still more eager that Blake and Tinker should get a good start. So she entered the cathedral and spent half an hour in her devotions. Then she came out and, calling up her sweetest expression, took herself back to the cuartel.

She arrived just in time to intrude upon a stormy scene that revealed Captain Gouffra in a not very attractive light. The gaoler had discovered that there was an elderly woman in the cell where the young prisoner, Juan Castro, should have been. He had rushed back to inform the captain of this amazing fact and the latter, conceited ass though he was, had sense enough to realise how they had been duped. He chose to forget that it was at his orders the visitor had been admitted to the cell. Like all his kidney, he blamed everything on his subordinate, and he was expressing his opinion in high-pitched language that made Carlotta put her fingers in her ears. It took some moments for Gouffra to swallow his choler enough to make some effort to appear calm.

"Your pardon, senorita, but a most amazing thing has happened. I am glad you are here. Perhaps you can explain—"

Carlotta laughed easily.

"I have come to explain and to retrieve my duenna," she said lightly, as if the whole thing was some harmless girlish prank. "And you are not going to be angry with me are you Jaime?"

His lids batted several times, but he made a pretence of being of a most indomitable mind.

"What have you to say—Carlotta?" he managed to get out. "This is a serious thing, as you must know. Even if you are daughter of the Minister of Finance, you are not permitted to tamper with the laws, and you have done an unheard of thing— you have caused a prisoner to be released. Do you know who that prisoner was?"

Her eyes widened. She knew now that Gouffra had read the report of the raid on the treasury and that, while he hadn't a notion of her reasons, he had a suspicion that there was a lot behind all this. But she played him like the fish he was.

"Why—Jaime," she stammered, her lovely eyes clouding. "I hope you are not suggesting that I—I, Carlotta Alvarez, do not know my duty to the State? Why make such a fuss over that poor, ignorant boy from the hills? He could not have done very wrong. And my poor duenna was so miserable. It can't matter much that we used a little—strategy to get him away. You would have done as much for your old nurse—Jaime."

She had him and he knew it. He hummed and hawed and strutted and frowned, but Carlotta kept tightening the line all the time, and at the psychological moment, she gaffed him.

"You don't wish me to remain here in this heat, I know, Jaime. Come to see me this evening and I will explain whatever you ask me. You will come, won't you— Jaime?" She hadn't the slightest intention, however, of being at the town house that evening. She was riding to the hacienda that same afternoon.

He capitulated and a few moments later the triumphant Carlotta left the cuartel once more, escorting this time the real duenna. The moment she was gone Captain Gouffra turned to the gaoler.

"You fix up something that will make it look as if he escaped," he said thickly. "And let me warn you, hombre, if this gets beyond these walls I'll have you broken and sent to the mines. Do you understand?"

The gaoler took one look at the hard, snaky eyes, then he saluted.

"Si, senor," he muttered. "It is as if it never happened."

CHAPTER 9.   Blake Greases the Skids for Don Cristofo.

THE sun was well up by the time Blake and Tinker emerged from the coulee, where the lad had shed the duenna's garments and started on foot for Don Fernando's hacienda. Like ninety-five per cent. of the people of the country they were barefooted—a condition that had proved useful when Tinker had donned the duenna's clothes, for if he had had to put on her shoes (had she worn any) there might have arisen a serious difficulty.

The soles of their feet had hardened considerably during the time they had been in San Jose, but even yet they were not "leathery" enough to withstand the sharp rubble of the hill country so, perforce, they had to choose a roundabout way in order to keep to the dusty mule tracks.

It was mid-day before they passed the crest of the hills and started down towards the immensely rich and fertile valleys, which terraced down for a thousand feet to the great pampas beyond.

There, before them, lay the real wealth of Santa Marta. No country could have asked for more prolific soil than that, and, had the government inaugurated a system of honest cultivation, there would have been no need to seek foreign loans.

Even as it was the valleys were masses of shining green, where the coffee plantations lay, and far in the distance, where the russet hue of the pampas stretched into the horizon, they knew that thousands of cattle roamed. It was a picture of Nature at her loveliest and richest, and as he paused to survey it Blake shook his head.

"What a beastly crying shame," he murmured to the lad. "Wealth before us, young 'un, sufficient to keep ten times the population in luxury and yet what is the actual condition? Nine-tenths of the population as poverty-stricken as it possibly can be; the other tenth fighting and grasping and stealing whatever they can. One day this will fall into the hands of those who will appreciate the bounties which Heaven has distributed here with such prodigal hand and then—"

Tinker nodded, the lad had an inborn love of the soil, and there was such beauty lying there before him—such warmth of loveliness pulsating beneath the warm tropic sun—that it hurt physically to think of it being used as nothing but a pawn by men who thought of it only in terms of pesos.

"What a plantation one could make over there, guv'nor," he remarked, waving his hand towards a rich, green and red valley to the right.

"There is a stream there, too, young 'un, though we can't see it from here. That, I think, is the outlying portion of Don Fernando's estate. We shall make for the stream and have something to eat there. I have a little food inside my shirt, and we ought to find some bananas."

They started on again, passing a peon now and then, but, considering the population the rich stretch of country ought to be carrying, it was almost deserted. A small valley led them to the larger one, and, as Blake had calculated from the configuration of the land, they came upon a lovely little stream which tumbled along between bush green banks with an eternal silver song.

They picked a shady spot under some bamboos, and when Tinker had beaten about to see if there were any snakes lurking near, they settled down to eat. Close at hand were bananas for the taking. Rather, were they plantains, for the true banana does not grow as high as that. There is a general idea that the plantain and the banana are one and the same. This is not so, although they belong to the same family, and are very close cousins.

As a matter of fact, the edible banana which comes from Central America and the West Indies is a large fruit known as the Gros Michel. This is the banana known in England as the "Jamaica," and, despite the partiality of the fruit dealers, is a much finer fruit than that which comes from the Canary Islands.

The Gros Michel did not exist forty years ago. It is what is known as a "sport," and is entirely sexless. Therefore, it is not propagated by pollen as are sex plants—which applies, too, to all other bananas. The Gros Michel was an accident, and from a single tree has been propagated by "bits" (that is the root which is cut in pieces, each bit containing one or more "eyes") in the same way the potato is cultivated. And now the banana, which began with that single sport, covers a tremendous area in Central America and the West Indies. This by the way.

What with the frijoles (beans of the country) and tortilla (pancakes) which Blake had brought, they managed with the plantains to make a fairly substantial meal, and when they had drunk deep from the stream they lay back in the shade to wait until the worst of the heat was past. They had covered a good half of the distance to the Alvarez hacienda, and as Blake had no wish to get there before nightfall there was no great hurry.

Blake smoked and talked in desultory fashion. He told the lad just how Carlotta had planned his release, and from that drifted on to speaking about their raid on the treasury.

"Everything depends on how Don Fernando acts now," he said, his eyes resting with lazy pleasure on the vast panorama which lay before them. "He sent for us to come here and dig up certain evidence and proof against the president. Well, we have done our part. We took evidence out of that safe last night that is sufficient to condemn Don Cristofo a dozen times over. I know exactly what that crook's game is now."

"What is it, guv'nor?"

"Don Cristofo doesn't care two straws about Santa Marta so long as he can line his pockets. The graft going on in this little republic is appalling, Tinker. And even Don Cristofo and his gang know it can't continue indefinitely. That is why they are so eager to clinch this new loan."

"You mean?"

"Just this—as soon as they get their hands on that money there will be a hasty division, and then—pouf! There will be a general fading away. Remember that bunch of American banknotes we saw in the safe last night?"

"I should say so—a small fortune."

"Quite so. That is part of Don Cristofo's 'getaway' money. He is not taking any chances. All his stuff is being turned into hard cash, so he won't be burdened with documents that are difficult to negotiate. I'll wager that crook has thousands more locked away in safety deposit in New York or London. It is in his mind to make one more big clean-up out of the new loan and then skip."

"He's a dirty dog, guv'nor."

"You've said it. He is worse. It doesn't matter to him that he will leave a lovely mess of chestnuts to be pulled out of the fire. He hasn't got a streak of loyalty in his make-up. Old Don Ruiz Mendoza, the dictator of a few years ago, was a hard nut, but he loved this country. Don Cristofo regards it simply as a cow to be milked."

"The Santa Martans are a sweet bunch of corral snakes," remarked Tinker.

"They are—the political pseudo-military crooks. There are a few exceptions, but not many. Don Fernando is straight, but fears the president's crowd. If he could only be bolstered up a bit he would be able to strike a telling blow. He could have the presidency to-morrow if he played a bold hand."

"Senorita Carlotta has nerve enough, anyway."

"She has. That girl is a jewel. If Don Fernando only had her courage the problem would be simple. I have a feeling that Carlotta is going to play even a bigger part in this before we finish. My heavens! If she were only of the other sex I'd put up a plot in this country that would have her in the president's chair before Don Cristofo knew what was happening. We need a strong candidate, young 'un!"

"You say 'we,' guv'nor," said Tinker, with a grin. "You talk as if we were Santa Martans."

Blake smiled.

"We may become Santa Martans for a brief time if the game is good enough, my lad. I'd give a good deal to take a proper fall out of Don Cristofo and his gang."

"What about General Primo de Miguel? I have heard him talked about here and there."

Blake made a gesture of contempt.

"Not worth a straw, young 'un. He's as weak as ditchwater, and as big a knave as Don Cristofo. He hasn't the brains of the latter, but he makes a good tool for those who are plotting to get into power before the new loan comes through. It is an unholy scramble with this poor, rich little country as the security for what those robbers can beg, borrow or steal. One good, straight man could get a stranglehold on the whole outfit if he acted boldly. And the bulk of the ordinary people want it. They are sick of being ground to the last colone—ay, the last rei for the benefit of the governing gang. But enough of politics. Let us get going. Something may suggest itself, and to-night we shall have Carlotta at the hacienda to put in her word as well."

Blake was right in thinking the valley which was watered by the stream was the outlying part of the Alvarez property. It was one of the largest haciendas in Santa Marta, beginning on that slope of the hills and stretching away for many miles across the table-land which was nearly all rich feeding pampas where thousands upon thousands of cattle roamed.

Don Fernando was a very wealthy man, and could have been

even richer if he had worked the whole property intensively. But without a son he had not the incentive. He knew that when he died Carlotta would be more than well provided for, and it was the great anxiety of his later years to find her a suitable husband. When he was gone Carlotta's husband would have full control of the great estates, for such is Spanish custom; and Don Fernando knew how quickly even that wealth could be frittered away in the wrong hands.

Still, Carlotta was a sensible girl, and not easily to be imposed upon. As a matter of fact, Carlotta was worth two of almost any young man one might pick at random in the country, but then, while he acknowledged she was an exceptional girl, Don Fernando could not cast off the prejudice of his race which accepted all women as distinctly inferior to the most useless men.

While he had not tried to persuade Carlotta to look with more favour on the suit of the president's son, he would have been secretly pleased if they had been betrothed, for, despite his strong belief that Don Cristofo was a crook, and was milking the country's funds at a terrific rate, he thought he was too firmly in the saddle to be unseated without such proof as seemed hopeless to seek. And even with that in his hands, Don Fernando would have hesitated just as Sexton Blake had figured.

He would keep the proof against a day when it might come in useful as a weapon of defence; but as an instrument of offence —well, he would need a lot of stirring up. When he had sent for Blake he had been acting under the heat of acute indignation. But with Blake's arrival he had realised what his own position would be if Don Cristofo discovered what was afoot; and when he looked across his broad acres— thought of his daughter whom he regaided as defenceless should anything happen to him—he hesitated.

This was exactly the situation which Blake had anticipated. He had witnessed the cooling off that had taken place in Don Fernando's ardour, and he knew the reason. But that did not cause Blake to lessen his efforts. On the contrary. He had put forward the date of his raid before Don Fernando should get cold feet to the extent of forbidding it. With actual proof in his possession, Blake would know better how to play his hand. And he hadn't the faintest intention now of dropping things.

He had been sent for to come there and do a certain job. He was going to complete that job whether Don Fernando wished to stop or not. Once he had a matter in hand Blake would never leave it at half-done. And when it was all over he would see that his fee was forthcoming from someone.

They took things easy so as not to arrive at the hacienda before dusk. Not that there was much risk, for, from what he had already learned, Blake knew that all the peons on the Alvarez estate could be trusted thoroughly not to betray any guests of their master.

He wanted, too, to give Carlotta a chance to arrive. He was anxious that she should be present when he talked things over with her father. She had, he reckoned, passed them during the afternoon, but as she would ride out by the road while they were sticking to little-travelled mule tracks, they would not see her. She had already sent word to the estancia that they were coming, and when they finally approached the great white-washed homestead they skirted the garden in order to try and get a glimpse of Don Fernando.

As Blake hoped, he was strolling up and down among the paths which cut through the rich tropical tangle, and at first he drew up in amazement at the two sorry-looking objects who approached him. He was a tall, thin man, almost jaundice-yellow of skin, but looking distinguished with the contrasting white Castillian beard and moustache and the heavy white hair which crowned him. He had been a fine, upright figure in his youth, but he stooped somewhat now, and his face wore a look of sadness which had been stamped there ever since Carlotta's mother had died.

"My daughter has already arrived," he said as he drew them along the path. "I have been on the look-out for you. But you will be quite safe here."

He conducted them on to a wide veranda, and from there through open French windows directly into the rooms they were to occupy. His own servant was on hand to look after them, and, when they had indulged in a bath and had donned the fresh white clothes which were provided for them, they both felt decidedly better.

Not that they removed the stain which had been the chief part of their disguise. This was still effective, but, just to be on the safe side, a fresh touch was put on here and there, and when they finally joined their host on the veranda in front they were, outwardly, the same Ramon Castro and his assistant who had arrived from Bogota a week or more before.

Carlotta, looking more delightful than ever in a soft, filmy white frock, was there with her father. Her eyes glinted with amusement as she greeted them demurely, and she laughed softly when she looked at Tinker. She could not forget the picture the lad had made as a sad and weeping duenna.

No mention was made yet of the business which had brought Blake out to the estancia. That, was, by unspoken consent, to be left until after dinner. Cocktails were brought out to them before they went in, for in all its domestic details the Alvarez household was run on the modern lines which Carlotta had introduced since being at school in Europe. Then they moved in to the great dining-room, where a large electric fan kept the air cool and pleasant.

During dinner the conversation ranged from one subject to another, but time and again it rested on the political gossip of the country. The name of Don Cristofo was left strictly alone, but even Don Fernando had to smile when Carlotta related the details of how she had fooled his son that morning. Afterwards, however, he frowned.

"The Gouffras can be bad enemies, chicita," he said soberly. "If Jaime discovers the truth he may turn nasty."

"Poof, papa! Who cares? I do not mind the Gouffras." Then her shapely little head went up proudly. "The Alvarez were in New Spain when the Gouffras were donkey drivers in Andalusia."

Don Fernando sighed, while Blake and Tinker mentally applauded the girl's spirit.

"That may be so, chicita, but we are living in to-day, and this is Santa Marta, of which Don Cristofo is president."

Carlotta shrugged and shifted the conversation. She shot a meaning look at Blake, who interpreted the signal correctly. Forthwith he changed the talk to a safer subject. This brought up the situation on the coast, and Don Fernando showed a sudden anxiety to discuss it.

"I have had letters to-day which seem to point to the existence of a good deal of unrest in Santa Marta city," he said slowly. "There is a lot of talk about General Primo de Miguel being in the country. If that is so, then there will be trouble."

"He was exiled, I believe," put in Blake.

"Yes; after his last attempt at the presidency. He has no very good following, but he can command the support of plenty of money in Santa Marta, and, of course, there is a large body ready to throw their weight to any side which promises the most pickings. I have heard, too, of the presence of a woman in Santa Marta, who is a most undesirable person. She has been in Santa Marta before. She possesses an uncanny power over the negroes and mestizos, and, as you know, the negro population on the coast is very large. The blacks and the mestizos form an element that has to be taken into consideration."

"A woman! One who wields great power over the blacks! I wonder if it can be the same woman of whom I know—though her activities are mostly among the islands of the Caribbean, mostly in Hayti."

"It may be the same. The woman I speak of comes from the islands. Her name is Marie Galante."

Blake laid down his knife and fork and stared at Don Fernando. Tinker was showing signs of excitement that puzzled Carlotta.

"Marie Galante!" exclaimed Blake. "It is the same. If that woman is plotting down in Santa Marta, senor, then you can expect real trouble before long. Where she goes the flag of intrigue waves. She will stop at nothing. Do you think she is in league with General Primo de Miguel?"

"My information indicates that," admitted Don Fernando cautiously. "But we shall speak of this after dinner."

Little more was said during the meal. Blake was mulling over in his mind this latest phase while Tinker, in a low tone, was telling Carlotta what he knew about Marie Galante. Don Fernando was as silent as Blake. The whole atmosphere was pregnant with the weight of intrigue which was abroad on the country, and which was gripping them even out here on the isolated estancia.

But once in the great living-room with coffee and cigarettes close at hand and the servants dismissed, Don Fernando seemed anxious to hear what Blake had to say. Briefly Blake gave him the details of the raid on the treasury, and when he had finished he took out the packet of evidence which he had brought away with him.

"Here is what you have been seeking, senor," he said quietly. "It is what I came to San Jose to find, and I have found it. There is that here which condemns Don Cristofo Gouffra over and over again. There is enough material here to impeach half a dozen presidents. Will you have it?"

Don Fernando took the thin packet and laid it on the low table beside him. He did not attempt to read it. Instead, he pulled at his pointed white beard.

"I will accept your words, senor," he said slowly. "But I know not what to say. I am uncertain how to act. If I make this public and call upon Don Cristofo to make restitution, I shall precipitate an upheaval the end of which no man can see. When I sent for you I knew nothing of the intrigue which is going on in Santa Marta. I thought the way would be clear. But if I come out now with this denunciation of Don Cristofo, it will touch off the powder of another revolution. The result might be worse than present conditions. It would, indeed, if Primo de Miguel got into the president's chair."

"But consider yourself, senor," said Blake quickly. "You could carry all the best elements of the country with you. It is you for whom the presidential chair is waiting."

"No, no. If it could be managed by a peaceful revolution, then I should do my duty. But not through blood. I am too old and I have seen enough welter in my poor country."

It was just as Blake had feared it might be. He shot a look at Carlotta to signal that she should take the lead if she thought best. But before she could speak her father was saying:

"I have been thinking all day, senor. It is a position which confounds me. I cannot think of a single person who would serve our purpose. We need another Ruiz Mendoza. He was hard and selfish, but just, and this position is just the sort he would straighten out. I have not the physical strength to face it, though heaven knows I would give my life willingly if it would serve my poor country. I do not know what to say."

Blake's eyes grew stern.

"Hear me, senor. You sent for me to come to San Jose and uncover a system of stealing which you suspected existed. I came and I have found a scandalous state of affairs. It isn't only the people of Santa Marta who are being robbed by the scoundrels who are in power. The foreign bondholders who have invested their good money in the securities of the country are being defrauded. Are you going to stand by while this new loan is floated and the money goes into the pockets of Cristofo Gouffra and his gang? Is it not our bound on duty to your country and to the foreign bondholders to come forward and speak the truth—truth which you can prove to the wide world with the papers which I have placed in your hands? If you do not do so, I tell you, senor, that I shall feel compelled to broadcast that truth to the world.

"Knowing what I do, I cannot stand by and see my own country people send their money here to become only the gambling stake of Cristofo Gouffra. If I do nothing else, I shall kill that loan. But that does not help what is gone. Time and again has Santa Marta repudiated the interest on the bonds already outstanding. Where is the money to come from to pay that? Is that bundle of banknotes which I saw in the president's private safe at the treasury to be allowed to form part of what he has stolen? Is he to be permitted to flee abroad, and take his ill-gotten gains with him? It would be a monstrous thing."

"No, father, no! It cannot be permitted."

It was Carlotta's clear voice which had rung out, and at the almost masculine decision in it—the echoing pride of honour of country—the old man winced.

"Be quiet, chicita," he said. "Let me consider our friend's words in all their bearings."

There was a long silence, during which Don Fernando sat with his head sunk on his chest, and hand shading his eyes from the light. His daughter's eyes were very soft and tender as she regarded him, but she did not go to him. She was determined that in some way Cristofo Gouffra should be exposed as what he was—that Blake's advice should be followed. In that moment she was wishing passionately that she had been son to Don Fernando instead of daughter.

At last her father raised his head.

"What you say is all true, senor," he said painfully. "Yet, think as I will, I can see no way. If you have something to suggest, I will consider it."

Blake, too, had been thinking hard; and now he answered:

"Please do not think that I do not understand your reasons for hesitating, senor. I shall, of course, do nothing precipitate. But if things are marching on the coast as you say, then something must break soon. You have said that you would make a definite stand if there was a leader to put forward."

"Yes—a man of integrity."

"Very well, we shall leave it at that for the present. I shall go down to Santa Marta and find out exactly what is going on there. Something may occur to me. I have no desire to cause an upheaval until I have an alternative to offer. But while I am there I can learn something, and, incidentally, I can arrange a net to catch Don Cristofo when he tries to leave the country. I am convinced that this is in his mind—that he will go as soon as he can lay his hands on a slice of the new loan which is being floated. And I am determined that he shall not take it away with him. For the rest, we must wait and see. Do you approve of this?"

"Yes, senor. You will keep me advised?"

"Naturally; and as soon as I see a way— if there is one to be found—I shall come to you and put it before you."

At that it was left, and after some further discussion it was arranged that Blake and Tinker should leave the hacienda at dawn the next morning, so as to catch the early train at San Jose for the coast. There was no chance to talk with Carlotta alone before they retired, but the following morning as Blake and Tinker stepped out on to the veranda, the girl came swiftly towards them through the morning mist. She caught each by an arm, and, gazing up into Blake's eyes, whispered:

"If there is anything—anything at all that I can do you will send for me, won't you? Promise me this before you go."

Blake laid his hand on hers.

"I promise, senorita. If there is anything in which you can help us, I shall not fail; I'd rather have your active assistance than that of anyone else in Santa Marta."

The girl flushed divinely at Blake's words, and then just before they left her she put a letter into Blake's hands.

"The person to whom this is addressed is my mother's brother. He is wild, and my father does not approve of him. But he is honest and full of courage. He knows Santa Marta as the palm of his hand, and may be of use to you. You will go to him?"

"Without fail, senorita."

"Then my mind will be easier. And now, God go with you, senores."

They left her then, a slim white wraith in the mist as they stepped off the veranda and passed through the garden to where the horses were waiting. They had said goodnight to Don Fernando the night before, so, swinging into the saddle, they set off at a steady lope for San Jose, little dreaming as they went along what lay in wait for them at Santa Marta.

CHAPTER 10.   Rymer Tackles Several Difficulties and Finds a Way Out of One.

HUXTON RYMER was on the horns of a dilemma.

He knew that Mary Trent was not the sort of girl to tolerate his association with Marie Galante for a single moment if she suspected the veriest fraction of the truth. His previous connection with the island woman had been kept a profound secret from Mary. It had never entered his head that the two could ever cross each other's path, for the simple reason that he intended to take pains to guard against it.

On the other hand, Marie Galante would be flamingly jealous of Mary as soon as she knew of her existence, and there was no telling what she might do if she guessed anything of the truth of the relations that existed between her and Rymer.

It may be said that Rymer deserved to get it in the neck for his duplicity, but, in fairness to the adventurer, it must be said that from the moment he had formed his association with Mary Trent, he had had nothing to do with any other of her sex, except on that one occasion in New York, when he had joined with Marie Galante in the plot against the Black Emperor; and then he had not been exactly a free agent.

But, aside from the ethics of the matter, the fact stood out stark and clear that he was in Santa Marta, his capital, staked on a gamble for some of the plums he figured were to be picked up in that country, Mary Trent with him, and, it seemed, the whole success of his plans was dependent on the "yes" or "no" of his old flame, Marie Galante. A pretty pickle, if you will.

What could he do? There was no denying the existence of Mary, for she was very much alive and very much on the scene. Nor could he pass off Marie Galante as someone he had just met and with whom he had joined forces for this occasion only. Both girls were far too quick to be fooled by such infantile stuff as that; and jealousy would quicken their wits.

Rymer knew that if Mary learned the truth she would pack up and clear out by the first available ship. And if she did go it would mean finis to their partnership. That was a thing he could not contemplate, no matter what happened, for the simple reason that he was passionately in love with Mary, just as she was with him. But he knew her nature, and he knew she would forgive anything but such an unpleasant reality as Marie Galante.

As for the latter, she was capable of anything. If she knew the truth she would not hesitate to visit some bodily harm upon Mary. In fact, Rymer realised that Mary's life would be in acute danger from the mulatto woman, for Marie Galante was a hot, exotic jungle primitive, who would stop at nothing. It was quite on the cards that he would be in danger as well, but that didn't worry him.

The thing to be faced was the actual problem which would arise if one discovered the truth—or even a portion—about the other. And Marie Galante held most of the trumps, for the simple reason that she was on her own ground, with every black on the coast literally her slave. A snap of the fingers would bring hundreds of killing knives at her service.

Nevertheless, Rymer thought there must be some way out. He did not want to give up his gamble for the presidency unless he was forced to, and he did not think this should be necessary. It smacked of weakness and cowardice to run because a couple of petticoats might start something, and he was hanged if he was going to do it.

Then there was young Mendoza, who depended on him to carry out his promises. Could he utilise him in some way in solving the problem? There was no doubt that Mendoza was very keen on Mary—or thought he was, at any rate—and if Marie Galante could be made to believe that he was a sort of guardian to Mary and that she favoured the suit of the young man, then everything might yet be lovely in the garden. That is, if Mary could be got to play up without knowing why she was doing so. She had done so on board ship, but then she had known the reason, and no other woman had entered into it.

Could he get her to continue the game, and keep from her the fact that it was necessary to play it on account of Marie Galante? There seemed no other way to go ahead, and he must if he was to make use of the organisation the mulatto woman had already built up.

This was what was seething in his mind all the next day after his conversation with Marie Galante. It is little wonder that both Mary Trent and young Ruiz Mendoza thought him strange—distrait. Rymer put them off by saying that he had a touch of temperature as, indeed, he had, but not from coast fever, as he had led them to believe.

He managed to get rid of them again that afternoon while he went to keep a rendezvous with Marie Galante. So far he had not hinted at the existence of the mulatto woman, he had simply said that he was on the track of important news, and things were moving as well as could be expected.

This was only one complicated problem which was looming before him. The next, and equally important, was the question of General Primo de Miguel. Rymer had already made up his mind that the seasoned old villain must be got rid of entirely. At first he had been inclined to concede a point, and permit him to take part as a subordinate to young Ruiz Mendoza—as chief of staff, or some other post of the sort where his self-importance might be pandered to, and yet he would not be able to interfere with the real progress of things. But that opened out too many difficulties, and Rymer realised that he would have to be got rid of entirely. But how?

Marie Galante was already pledged to the fellow. All her preliminary work had been done with Primo de Miguel held up as the next president of Santa Marta. His name had already been incorporated in half a dozen slogans which were being circulated quietly among the people.

Everything had been directed to the point where General Primo de Miguel would be called for on every side when the gage was thrown down. If he were eliminated all that work would have to be done over again, and, ordinarily, Rymer would have agreed that it was scarcely possible to whip up enthusiasm a second time for the purposes of a revolution.

But his own candidate was no ordinary person. He counted on bringing forth young Mendoza at a moment when the name of the former dictator should be in everybody's mouth. A little judicious propoganda would soon prepare the way for that. The people were in the sort of mood now when all the old dictator's virtues were being remembered, and his faults forgotten.

If Juan Ruiz Alarcon y Mendoza could be suddenly put before them while those refulgent rays played about him the people would seize upon the idea with avidity, and on the wave of the terrific enthusiasm which would follow his candidate would be swept into office. So Rymer figured. But there again he had to buck the obstinacy of Marie Galante. She was a person who knew her own mind, and she was not taking kindly to the idea of scrapping all her own plans and throwing herself heart and soul into Rymer's scheme.

If it hadn't been Rymer she would have scorned the suggestion.

But Rymer was Rymer, and the mulatto woman went weak at the knees when he was with her. She stormed at herself inwardly for not being strong enough to withstand him, but that didn't change it.

He was the only man who had ever affected her in this way, and when his voice sounded caressingly in her ears every atom of hot blood that coursed within her seemed to concentrate in her heart until it swelled to bursting-point. If that emotion was ever roused by rage against him, then Heaven help Rymer.

The adventurer made his way in the direction of the wine shop by a route that took him through the plaza and down by the market. He chose this longer route in order to keep Mary in ignorance of his destination in case she and Mendoza should be walking that way. He did not skirt the market, but walked through the centre between the dirty stalls, where every fly in Santa Marta seemed to have congregated in an orgy about the withered remains of fruit and vegetables which still were to be sold.

The odour offended his fastidious nostrils exceedingly, but that was far less offensive than things would be if his plans went wrong, for he might well find himself in a Santa Martan gaol, than which nothing could be more noisome.

The lower end of the market came out close to the river bank, for it was by water that a good deal of the produce arrived each morning. There was a wide revetment here, and, turning to the right, Rymer picked his way past individual stalls until he reached a narrow, dirty road beyond. This led him to the wine shop, and as soon as he reached the door he slipped in quickly.

The place was deserted. He could not see a soul through the gloom, but when he made his way to the room at the back he saw Marie Galante sitting at the table, her head cupped in both hands. She watched him with shadowed eyes as he removed his sun-hat and gave her a cheery greeting. He felt a twinge of uneasiness when she did not respond, but acted as if everything was quite all right. He seated himself opposite her, and, after smiling into her eyes, ventured:

"Well, been thinking over what I said?"

"Let that wait. Who is the girl at the hotel with you?"

It had come. How she had discovered Mary's presence so soon was a mystery to Rymer, unless she had lost no time in setting spies to dog his every movement. But the question had to be answered.

"The girl at the hotel with me?" he echoed, frowning as if in

74

concentration. Then: "Oh! You must mean Miss Trent— Mary Trent!"

"That is her name," came in low, sombre tones from which hot jealousy was literally dripping. "You have not answered my question. What is she doing travelling with you? What is she to you?"

"For Heaven's sake don't get worked up over Mary," protested Rymer, with a laugh which he tried to make light. "She—why, she is just travelling with me. I am her guardian in a way. A nice girl, too; you would like her. She knows that I sometimes take a flier that runs close to the law, but she thinks it is all right. She— or—there seems to be quite an affair developing between her and young Mendoza. It would be a joke if I made him president and he married her."

She rose swiftly and leant across the table. One hand gripped his like a vice, and her hot breath was on him as she fixed him with her burning eyes. She was like a panther whose "kill" is threatened. Slowly she put one hand to her bosom, and then it came back even more slowly until it was hovering over the table. She opened her fingers, and a silver-hilted dagger dropped with a clatter on to the mahogany. Rymer eyed it in fascination.

"If she is anything to you, I will bury that dagger in her heart!" she hissed.

She straightened up, and swept into the front shop. Rymer, wiping the sweat from his brow, could hear her moving about; but he did not follow. At the same time he eased his chair back a little so he could come into action quickly if necessary. But there was to be no need. At the end of ten minutes or so the mulatto woman returned, and now her emotion seemed to have passed, although her slumbrous eyes were heavy and the lids drooped as if weighted.

"I have been thinking about what you said," she remarked quietly, as if a terrific explosion had not been imminent a few minutes before. "What do you suggest about de Miguel?"

Rymer breathed easier. He did not pretend to understand why she had chosen to drop the subject of Mary, but far be it from him to reopen it. He sensed that the fires were smouldering just the same, and he knew that smouldering flames have a habit of bursting out when one least expects them. But he would not meet trouble halfway.

"I still adhere to what I said," he answered easily. "If you adopt my plan then he will be only an encumbrance. He hasn't any real following, anyway. He might occupy a certain position because you put him in it, but that bunch up in San Jose isn't going to let him get away with the goods without putting up an awful fight. If I didn't have someone like young Mendoza I should say let us use de Miguel, and make the best of it. But my judgment is sound in this, Marie. Let us scrap him."

"How?"

"Clear him out of the country."

She was thoughtful for a little.

"That is easier said than done," she answered at last. "He is not altogether at my disposal. You must know that in order to put this thing through, and get the following I needed here, I had to bring in a certain element here in Santa Marta. They will all want their pickings and de Miguel has a good many friends among them. They know that with him in power their pickings are certain. This young Mendoza is a stranger to them. What would you do if he suddenly developed scruples?"

There was a shrewd mind behind that question, and Rymer recognised it.

"He might if he fell under the wrong influence." he admitted. "Still, I think I am capable of guarding against that. When I am away he is in good hands."

A sneer curled her red lips, but she suppressed what she might have said about Mary.

"Look here, Marie." he went on persuasively, "be guided by me in this. You know that I would not advise making a clean sweep of de Miguel unless I felt certain my candidate would be much stronger. And, don't forgot, the very name will carry the people with him. I'll guarantee that de Miguel's friends won't be let down when the share-out comes."

"Very well. I'll give in on this. What do you propose. Have you any definite plan? We can't just tell de Miguel that we are dropping him. He would raise an awful rumpus and give the whole show away. If we drop him he must be silenced. I could arrange that easily enough," she added meaningly, "but it would not be wise."

"I have a perfectly safe plan—if I can lay my hands on him," put in Rymer. "I'll get him out of the country altogether, and once he is out I'll arrange that he shall not come in again until this show is over. Where is he now?"

"In hiding with friends,"

"Can you get him here—alone?"

"Yes, I could manage that. He will do as I say."

Rymer knew that she meant the physical appeal of her had enslaved the Spaniard, but he said nothing on that score. It was enough for him if she got the fellow there where he could deal with him. He didn't care what methods were used.

"When?"

"When you wish. To-night?"

"We can't move too soon. But I don't know if I can manage the other details by then. You might help."

"What do you need?"

"A craft of some sort. This is my plan. Have a schooner or some similar type of island craft ready. It could he moored at the jetty back of the wine shop. I'll see that Primo de Miguel is put on board. Then run him out to sea. Once he is out in the Caribbean I'll guarantee he doesn't come back. An anonymous tip to the port officials at Dos Hermanos will settle that. Then the boards will be clear."

She nodded her head, and her passionate eyes glinted into his. Rymer had her tuned perfectly now, and she was responding to the touch of this man, whose domination she liked against her will.

"I'll do that; and I can get hold of a craft. That negro who was in here yesterday. I have him under lock and key at present. He came in a small schooner. He will be only too glad to get away without undergoing what was promised him. I'll have him warp his boat in here this evening and be ready. What time do you suggest?"

"I'll come here at ten o'clock. Better have the place clear by then. As soon as I come in I'll tackle de Miguel. You leave that to me."

"Very well. After, we can talk again. That is enough for this afternoon. Come through into the private quarters with me now. I will make you some sherbet."[i]

And Rymer, although he would much rather have returned at once to the hotel— would have done almost anything to avoid a sentimental tete-a-tete with her—could not refuse. The slightest hint of such a thing would have caused those smouldering flames to burst out again. So he smiled as if he welcomed the suggestion, and followed her meekly, Rymer was getting in deeper and deeper.

It was after six o'clock when he got back to the hotel. Mary and Mendoza had been back some time and he found them seated in big cane chairs in the patio. He was hot and in a savage mood, but he smiled as if he hadn't a care in the world. Seating himself he listened to Mary's desultory relation of what they had done; then, after a glance round, he said in a low tone:

"I have had a busy time. Things are beginning to march. The docks will be clear to-night, and then, my boy, it will be time for you to meet some of your supporters. We shall lose no time, but strike while the iron is hot. How does that suit you?"

Ruiz Mendoza smiled. Ever since his arrival in Santa Marta he had befell drinking in the atmosphere of his native land. On every side he had found statues and other tributes to his father. He was becoming exalted in mind at the thought that, like his sire, he would come forth as the deliverer of his people.

Not a shred of greed was there in his nature. His ideas were all heroic, and if he had guessed the least part of all the intrigue that was going on about him he would have found it hateful. Just what Marie Galante had suggested to Rymer was beginning to struggle for expression in the young fellow. And be it said of Mary that she had not tried to quench it. She was an odd little mixture was Mary Trent.

"It can't come too soon for me," he said softly. "I am eager to meet those who will support me. I want them to know that I shall carry faith and decency into the government of this country. All the abuses which are rampant shall be swept away. And you, dear friend, will stand at my right hand."

An acute twinge of conscience surprised Rymer as Mendoza smiled at him. This was getting altogether too serious. He should have to speak to Mary and see that she kept his mind off such serious thoughts. He would have to be handled delicately, that was certain. Later, when he and Mary were alone in their private sitting-room before dinner, he referred to the matter. He had half-intended speaking of Marie Galante, but decided to let that wait until the events of the night were over.

He thought, he had used sufficient diplomacy to keep the mulatto woman quiet for the present, but, just the same, he was getting so nervy under the strain that every time a servant passed the slatted door of the room he turned sharply. Mary saw his state and wondered; but she knew whatever it was it would all come out in good time.

She explained what she thought was the reason young Mendoza was getting filled with such exalted thoughts, and she hit the truth. When she had finished, her lovely eyes sought Rymer's.

"I almost wish we had never come here," she said softly. "It seems not fair to trifle with the fine patriotism which fills the boy. I warn you now, old boy, that if he learns the truth you will never handle him."

"If he learns it then if will only be through you." he said a trifle snappishly.

Her face clouded, and she came to him quickly. Laying her hands on his broad shoulders she looked up into his eyes.

"What is it, old boy?" she asked, in a whisper. "You are not yourself. Tell me. You know you can trust me and that nothing matters to me."

He groaned inwardly. If he only could tell her. She said that nothing mattered to her, but little did she guess the truth. What would she think if she guessed that he had had to philander with another woman not two hours ago because her life was in danger. He cursed the impulse that had brought him to Santa Marta, but then he cursed himself anew for being weak. He was in this game—he would stick to the finish, and by the holy smoke he would win out. But Mary—

Suddenly he seized her fiercely, brutally. His head went down, and he pressed his lips against hers until she moaned with the hurt. Then he put her from him, saying unsteadily as he did so:

"Whatever happens you will stick, Mary? No matter what the test, you will not fail me?"

She laughed softly, one hand pressing against her bruised lips— lips that were tingling with a hurt that she loved.

"I'll stick—always, old boy—no matter what happens."

CHAPTER 11.   Rymer Eliminates General Primo de Miguel.

WHEN Rymer arrived once more at the wine shop he found that Marie Galante had followed his advice. The place was empty in the front, and the door leading into the back room was closed. A single oil lamp burned in the shop, and as soon as he stepped in the mulatto woman came through a curtained opening back of the counter.

Rymer raised his eyebrows questioningly, and she nodded. Then she bent over the counter, saying loudly in Spanish:

"We cannot serve anyone now, senor. The place is closed. Come to-morrow." Then in a whisper she added: "He is here, but has not come alone. A friend is with him."

Rymer nodded briefly and started for the heavy mahogany door that stood between him and the back room. In passing, it may be said that in Santa Marta as in several other Spanish American countries, mahogany is used as commonly as deal is employed in England, and there are rough floor and ceiling boards laid in dingy hovels of such beautiful graining that a cabinet-maker's eyes would glitter to see them.

Rymer had not dared to detain Marie long enough to ascertain further particulars. Had he done so those in the back room would probably have become suspicious, for every word spoken in a normal tone could be heard through the partition, while even the sibilant sound of whispers would carry.

Yet her warning that Primo de Miguel was not alone immediately complicated matters. If he had a friend with him, then that person would have to be dealt with as well. But supposing it were some prominent citizen of Santa Marta? Rymer would, in that case, have to decide quickly what to do, and whatever plan he adopted he would have to tread very gently.

The two men seated at the table turned their heads sharply as he pushed open the door and entered. Before they could speak Rymer had closed the mahogany panel and was standing with his back to it. The man nearest him was Primo de Miguel, he knew —a middle-aged, swarthy man who obviously had plenty of Indian blood flowing in his veins.

The other was an individual Rymer recognised at once as being a man he had seen about the town ever since his arrival. He was a heavily-built man of even darker line than the general. Bold eyes glittered above a broad, heavy nose, and a thick, cruel sensual mouth was only partially concealed by a sweeping black moustache. He looked like a nasty customer, and he was just that as Rymer knew.

The previous day, when the fellow had sat in the lounge at the hotel, Rymer had inquired about him. He had gathered that he was one Julio Bustro, a soldier of fortune, bully and gambler, who was notorious throughout Santa Marta as having taken part in half-a-dozen revolutions, managing each time to be on the winning side; and who had gained a certain unenviable reputation as a "killer." This was the bodyguard Primo de Miguel had chosen to accompany him—for as that and nothing else Rymer knew Bustro was there.

The "killer's" black, evil eyes were fixed upon Rymer in a menacing way. He had seen this immaculately-clad stranger with the well-trimmed pointed beard and now he was wondering what he was doing here in the wine shop. Marie Galante's words had been perfectly audible in the back room, and Bustro had taken it for granted that whoever entered the place had been sent about his business.

He was as sucpicious as an ocelot, and— as dangerous. Moreover, Julio Bustro had cast eyes of desire on the mulatto woman since he had seen her, and it grated on him to find that anyone else dared to push a way into that back room when he was there.

Rymer stared him down, and then coolly and deliberately he turned his back. There was a slight click as he locked the door, and at this sound the general gave an exclamation of amazement, while Bustro came to his feet with an oath. So far, Marie Galante had remained out of sight.

"Caramba!" snarled Bustro. "Who are you, and what do you mean by intruding here?"

Rymer dropped the key in the side pocket of his white jacket and smiled. His keen eyes noted that a long-bladed knife was stuck in Bustro's belt, while a pistol holster was slung round his waist, hanging low over the right thigh.

"Good-evening, senores," he said evenly. "Permit me to pay my respects to you, General de Miguel. I hoped I should find you here— alone, for I have something of importance to say to you. However, I presume I may speak in front of your servant."

"Servant!"

The "killer" spat the word out as if it were offal. He pushed behind the general and stood facing Rymer. He—Julio Bustro —the uncrowned king of the coast—the man at whose frown the worst characters in Santa Marta cringed—he whose gun butt contained more than a score of notches to record his killings—to be called servant to any man.

Only the death of him who used the word could wipe out that insult. His eyes were mere pinpoints of flame as he glared at Rymer. Just then he was telling himself that this gringo would die where he stood before another twenty seconds were passed.

And still the bearded adventurer just smiled. He looked quite relaxed in every way. He was—outwardly, but his eyes were very wary and he did not miss the slight pushing of Bustro's elbow as he got ready to claw at his gun. Rymer knew those signs too well. As they stood thus the curtain in one corner moved and Marie Galante stood in the opening watching them. Her eyes went from Bustro to Rymer, and then back again to Bustro.

She knew the man was on the verge of killing. She had seen men in the crescendo of passion too often to be mistaken. And she knew that Bustro was enamoured of her. To her he was an anathema. No matter what her own origin might be, Marie Galante was a woman who demanded only the best, and she had had a catholic experience of men. A greasy creature like Bustro could never have got within miles of her, particularly after she had known such a man as Huxlon Rymer.

Her hand went slowly to the bosom of the clinging, crimson shawl that was wound round her body and hips, revealing every sinuous line of the body. Her fingers curled round the pearl butt of a small, but effective revolver, and she waited. If Bustro did kill Rymer he would not live long to enjoy his triumph. That was a dead certainty. And thus she stood watching.

She would not interfere unless she had to. Rymer could look after himself, she knew, and she had no doubt of the outcome of any struggle between those two unless Bustro should shoot without warning.

"You filthy gringo," burst out Bustro. "You—scum of the gutter, dare to call me, Julio Bustro, servant. You will eat those words on your knees, hear me, or I'll open up your heart with lead. You cannot know of whom you spoke."

"On, I know about you," drawled Rymer. "You are Julio Bustro—a boasting windbag. You think you are a 'killer.' Pah! You greasy frog, you never yet killed a man in fair fight and when you did kill one you stabbed him in the back. I know enough about you—greaser. As for you opening up my heart with lead—pah! Go ahead and see how far you will get with that boast."

"By—"

Bustro was insane with rage. Never in his life had he been insulted and flouted in this fashion. When he chose to assert himself men were acustomed to cringe. And, above all, to have his words thrown back at him in front of the woman.

His elbow straightened out as his hand went like lightning for his gun. His fingers slid round the butt and it was half out of the holster when Rymer reached him. Rymer had a weapon of his owm but he had not drawn it. He went for his man with bare hands, and a terrific straight right caught Bustro full in the throat. The kick behind it lifted him clean off his feet and slammed him back against the wall with such force that the whole building shook. He stood choking and gasping, for Rymer's fist had jammed his windpipe flat, bruising the larynx in a way that would keep the vocal chords paralysed for days. Nor did he leave it at that.

As Bustro lurched forward, still tugging wildly at his gun, Rymer jumped for him, stood only a foot or so away, and then with beautiful precision sent in a hard short left to the solar plexus.

Bustro doubled up like a jack-knife. A deep groan came from him as every shred of air was shot out of his lungs and he slid to the floor at Rymer's feet.

All this time General Primo de Miguel, the "hope" of the revolutionists, had remained seated, staring agape at the swift march of events. But now his naturally slow wits began to work and he came to his feet, trying to bluster in the face of this domineering stranger. He was uneasy, as well as puzzled. He was remembering that on entering, Rymer had said he had come to speak to him. What could he have to say? Who was he, anyway? And why was the mulatto woman smiling in such strange fashion?

"Senor," he fumed. "What is the meaning of this outrage? Why have you made this unprovoked assault upon my aide-de-camp?"

Rymer laughed outright. The general was bristling like a turkey cock. Rymer could have throttled him with one hand.

"Don't get excited, General," he said easily. "I am sorry that I found it necessary to treat your bodyguard in such fashion. But you must have seen that he was trying to get his gun out and he threatened to kill me. Therefore it was necessary to teach him a lesson. As for what I have to say to you, senor, it will not take long. I have some bad news for you."

"Bad news, senor," stuttered de Miguel, "what do you mean?"

"I regret to inform you, General, that it is impossible for you to continue as candidate for the presidency of Santa Marta. You must give way to another."

"Give way to another! Abandon the campaign! What de you mean, senor? How dare you talk to me in this fashion? I am General Primo de Miguel, commander-in-chief of the revolutionary army of the republic which will soon dominate the country. I shall have you shot, senor, for these insults. Woman," he shouted at Marie Galante, "what means this? Who is this person whom you have admitted?"

"Ask him," drawled the mulatto woman, who had eyes only on Rymer. It was this way he had of handling matters that always appealed to her. She was utterly ruthless herself, and only a man who could carry through things as Rymer carried them through could ever control her. But when she did yield she went the limit with all her jungle ferocity of passion.

Rymer put out one hand, and sent the general to his seat with a thud.

"I told you not to get excited," he said coldly. "I will explain more clearly. You are not commander-in-chief of anything; nor will you be. Your dream is over, general. You are a crooked old filibusterer who must get out of the game. Is that clear enough?"

"F-filibusterer! How dare you, you gringo scum! I, General Primo de Miguel! Filibusterer! You shall suffer for this, gringo. It is you who are worse than filibusterer!"

"Certainly," agreed Rymer easily. "We are both tarred with the same brush. I'm sitting in to the same game, general, and it is bad luck for you that you are going to miss those pickings. But it can't be helped. You've drawn a losing hand, and must get out. And I am here to see that you do get out. Get ready, senor—we move at once."

The swarthy skin of the other turned grey. All his cheap pomposity faded away. He saw all his dreams of wealth disappearing into mist. His fingers that had been ready to claw at the wealth which would fall under the control of the president of the country grew dry. He knew this big man who faced him was not bluffing. He knew in this moment that he meant every word he said—that he was to be kicked out of the game. And at that realisation he went crazy.

Springing to his feet, he opened his lips and started to mouth a stream of appalling curses. He got out one sentence before Rymer's hands were at his throat. Then the adventurer shook him like a terrier would flip a rat about, and when he had reduced him to a quivering mass he threw him bodily back into his chair. He bent over him until his hard, grey eyes bored into his very brain.

"Another spasm of that, you crooked old beast, and I'll tear your tongue out. Now control yourself. In just one minute you come with me."

The general, thoroughly shaken and cowed, threw a helpless look at his still unconscious bodyguard, then he slumped back with closed eyes. If a chance ever came he would have this devil before him put to a torture that would drag out his life interminably, but just now he could do nothing but bide his time. He little knew how literally Rymer meant that he was to be put out of the game.

Rymer signed to Marie Galante to bring a bottle of wine. When she had done so, he took a deep drink himself, then he thrust the bottle at the general.

"Take some," be ordered. "You'll need it before the night is over."

The other obeyed mechanically, and, while he was guzzling the liquid, Rymer raised his brows in a mute question to Marie Galante. The woman nodded.

"Everything is ready. The schooner can get away under the power of its own auxiliary engine. There is a small channel to the east of the sand-banks where he can slip through without being seen by the officials at Dos Hermanos."

"Good. You can trust him?"

"He will not fail. He is only too glad of a reprieve, and he knows what will happen to him if he plays any tricks."

Rymer nodded and turned back to the general. Reaching out, he took the bottle away from him.

"Get up," he ordered curtly. "We are ready to start."

"W-where are we going?" quavered the general. "Am I to be taken to some place away from my friends? You cannot commit this outrage, senor."

"Listen. There is a schooner at the jetty outside. You are going on that. As soon as you are out in the Caribbean you will be landed at any island you choose—if the people there will permit you to do so. If you try to slip back into Santa Marta you will get nabbed, for as soon as you are away I am going to see that the authorities know you have been here, are told that you have left, but may try to return. You will stay away until the revolution is over. Then—we shall see if you may return. That it all. Now come on."

There was nothing for it but to obey, the old crook who had been licking his lips at the thought of the rich pickings he was to get from the miserable, poverty-stricken peons of the country, was going out with empty pockets, and Huxton Rymer did not even try to bluff him that he was doing it out of any regard for the people of the country.

He owned that it was a case of "dog eat dog," and that made the other sicker than ever. But he had had sufficient reason not to resist. With Rymer gripping him hard and muttering threats in his ear of what would happen to him if he tried to call out, he was pushed through a door and down the stairs to the jetty.

At the end a small island schooner was moored, and when Marie Galante had sent a low hail over the side, the same giant negro whom Rymer had already manhandled appeared. He showed white teeth in a grin as he recognised the white man, and vowed his eternal loyalty as he grabbed the general and hauled him over the side.

They heard the prisoner being slung down into the hold, then Rymer returned for Julio Bustro. The latter was to be sent with the general, and Rymer grinned when he thought of the language there would be on the schooner when he came to his senses to find himself at sea.

He carried him bodily from the wine shop to the schooner, and gave ear with consideration to the bumps that sounded as he was heaved into the hold after his companion. He stood on the jetty with Marie Galante while the hatch cover was put on, and each threw off a rope as the negro whispered that he was ready. There followed the sputter of the auxiliary engine, and, after grinding against the jetty, the schooner slid off down the stream.

Thus did Rymer dispose of one problem. But there was still the difficulty of the two girls to be handled, and, unknown to him, there was approaching from San Jose, the capital, a still greater problem— one which was going to dwarf all other things.

CHAPTER 12.   Blake and Tinker Get a Dramatic Surprise.

BLAKE and Tinker kept both eyes and ears open when they rode into San Jose. It was then nearly eight o'clock in the morning, and they knew there had now been plenty of time for the news of the raid on the treasury to be conveyed to Don Cristofo. It was unlikely that he would be disturbed before his morning coffee was taken to him.

If the president feared for his own private papers in the treasury building, it was on the cards that he would lose no time in making an investigation, and, if he found such damning evidence missing as Blake had purloined, then he would turn San Jose inside out in order to regain his property.

In that case it would not be easy for Blake and Tinker to leave by the morning train. The fact that the accountant, Ramon Castro, and his assistant, were going away on the morning following the raid, might rouse suspicion against them. Of course, no search now would discover the missing documents on them, because they were safe in Don Fernando's possession.

But a close scrutiny might connect up the spruce-looking young clerk who accompanied Ramon Castro with the same lad who was found in the grounds of the treasury in the night. If Captain Gouffra was a fool, that epithet could not be applied to his father, who was as cunning an old fox as ever was cubbed. He would see no joke in the manner in which the prisoner of the cuartel had been released, particularly if he found out that some of his private papers had vanished in the raid. That is, if he learned from his son how Carlotta and her duenna had fooled him.

But Blake had a hunch that young Gouffra would not be at all anxious to publish this proof of his asininity. Nevertheless, no matter what yarn the son cooked up to explain the escape of the prisoner, the president might attach no little importance to the whole episode, and if there was a fine-tooth combing of the town, then Tinker must come into the net.

In that case they could only make a break for the open country if they got a chance, and make their way coastwards on foot by little-used paths.

The town, however, appeared perfectly normal. They rode right past the treasury, and, gazing in, they could certainly see a larger number of persons about than was usual at that hour of the morning.

There was going on, no doubt, a thorough examination in order to discover just what the intruders had been after.

With a sudden impulse Blake reined in and dismounted. He gave his bridle-rein to Tinker, and boldly strode up the path to the building. Tinker, amazed at this sudden move, could only watch, and wait, wondering what on earth was in Blake's mind. Considering what had happened the night before, he was not at all keen to remain out there to be scrutinised by anyone who passed.

But nothing out of the way had happened when, some ten minutes later, Blake reappeared. He walked down the path nonchalantly and swung himself into the saddle. Then he heeled his pony into a trot—an action which Tinker copied. But when they were through the plaza and nearing the market, Blake pushed his horse in close to the lad's animal.

"It seems all right so far," he said, in a low tone. "The president has been told, but hasn't come yet to investigate. Word has also been sent out to Don Fernando. The president may wait until he sees him, but that is only a guess. I saw the permanent secretary, and informed him that I should not be working on the books for a day or two. He did not seem to think it out of the way. That is one good thing about a country where everyone is so lazy. So it looks as if we might get away without any trouble. We shall make for the station, anyway. There is about half an hour before the train goes."

They rode on to the railway station—an unpretentious building of stone, where a train left once a day for Palma, which was on the river, about half-way to the coast, and into which a daily train arrived from the same place. There was no through railway to Santa Marta, the journey after Palma being completed by flat-bottomed river steamers of a very antiquated type.

A peon who had preceded them into San Jose was waiting at the station to take charge of the horses, so, when they had tossed him the bridle-reins, they entered a dirty little room called a restaurant and ordered coffee. At the same time Blake bought a morning paper. This was the one news sheet which appeared in San Jose, and he knew that such an affair as that which had taken place the night before would be played up by the editor for all it was worth.

When they were on the train, he opened the sheet, and there, sure enough, was a lurid account—as furnished by the night watchman— of the raid. Judging from what was written, it would seem that not less than a dozen desperate bandits had entered the place, and that, after a terrific struggle in the grounds, had shot their way to freedom, with the exception of one young fellow who had been captured. It was a good effort—not unlike the style of some journals in other countries.

From that Blake went on to read what was said about the escape of this same prisoner from the cuartel. And when he saw the tale that had been cooked up by young Gouffra, he certainly had to hand it to him as possessing a fertile mind that should have revealed itself when Carlotta was humbugging him.

For, from this account—which was endorsed by the gaoler—it would seem that the same desperate gang that had raided the treasury had returned to the town to rescue their young comrade. They had ridden to the cuartel just after the officer of the day—the paper stated that this was none other than the president's son, Captain Gouffra— had arrived; that after a struggle they had succeeded in overcoming Captain Gouffra and the gaoler, and had rescued the imprisoned member of the gang. It was an even better effort than the other, and Blake had to laugh as he handed the paper to Tinker.

At that moment the whistle went, and after many "vamanoses" had been yelled by the guard, the train started. Blake breathed easier. It was not likely now that they would be held up. They should be at Palma by late afternoon, and once aboard the river boat they would have little to fear before reaching Santa Marta.

Once they were in the coast town he figured they could do a lot of dodging before they were laid by the heels. Besides, he had that letter to Carlotta's uncle which might prove useful.

It was a beautiful run down through the gorges to Palma, which they reached late that afternoon. Naturally Blake and Tinker were on the qui-vive as they stepped out of the train and made their way along a rough track between scattered adobe huts to the dilapidated jetty where the river boat lay waiting. Palma is not a choice spot at any time, and at that time of the year it seemed to smell just a little worse than usual.

But no one accosted them except the soldier in brown cotton who stood at the gangway. He simply scrutinized their papers, and permitted them to go aboard. Still, Blake was restless until they finally got away, and then he breathed easier. They were all that night and the next day travelling down the river. It was almost dusk when they arrived at Santa Marta, and the swift tropic night was upon them before they got away from the jetty.

A roll of necessities had been thrown across each horse at Don Fernando's estancia, so, with this light luggage, they drove to the Pension Inglesa. Little did they dream that Huxton Rymer and Mary Trent were staying at the same hotel—the only possible one for Europeans in the place —nor of Rymer's activities the previous night, when he had run General Primo de Miguel out of the country.

Therefore, when they walked into the patio and took a table at one side, they got a considerable shock when they saw the adventurer, the girl, and a red-headed youth sitting at a table on the other side of the patio.

Rymer was side face to them, and so was the red-headed youth; but Mary Trent was facing them, and, despite the deep stain which they wore as well as the straggly beard which Blake had allowed to grow during the past week, the latter was not at all easy in his mind. He knew that Mary Trent was keen-eyed, and when, out of the corner of his eye, he saw her bend forward and say something to Rymer in what seemed low, urgent tones, he was wondering if she had pierced their disguises.

Not that he considered it of very great importance even if she had, for, of course, she had not the slightest suspicion that Rymer was mixed up in the intrigue which was seething in the coast town. He was to learn quite a lot before that night was over.

If Mary had told Rymer anything about the two newcomers, the latter gave no sign, but went on talking and laughing with the young man who sat opposite. From his manner, Blake could tell that he was putting himself out to impress and please his visa-vis, and he wondered just what game Rymer could have on.

He did not give much thought to that, however, for his mind was occupied with other matters, and as soon as he and Tinker had finished they went out at once to the lobby. There Blake made inquiries where he could find Senor Jose Guitterez. This was the name which Carlotta had written on the letter she had given him.

It seemed there would be no difficulty about that, for the gentleman appeared to be very well known. Detailed instructions were given to Blake how to reach his house, and with that information under his hat, he and Tinker started out, just as Rymer and his two companions emerged from the patio.

Senor Guitterez's house was, like those of other prominent

citizens, as close to the plaza as possible. It was a big place for Santa Marta, rambling and gloomy-looking, with, of course, a high wall all round it. The great wooden doors were closed, as usual; but, in answer to Blake's summons, a small wicket was opened by a peon, who, when he heard their inquiry, ushered them into a patio that was a perfect riot of green foliage and scented blooms. It seemed that, wild though he might be and frowned upon by Don Fernando though he was, Carlotta's uncle was a man of considerable wealth. This home of his was undoubtedly one of the finest mansions in Santa Marta.

He came to them soon—a robust man of medium height, and with a cast of countenance faintly reminiscent of Carlotta. He was dressed in white linen, the coat being fashioned as a dinner-jacket. He greeted them pleasantly, eyeing them a little curiously.

He seemed surprised when Blake bowed, and, after introducing himself as Ramon Castro, passed him Carlotta's letter. But, as soon as he read that, his manner became distinctly cordial. He led them to one corner of the patio, where white wicker chairs were placed, and, clapping his hands for a peon, sent the man scuttling off to bring drinks and smokes. Then he turned a pair of shrewd eyes on Blake.

"My niece tells me you have a secret to confide in me, senor. Her word is law to me. She is the child of my dear sister, and is my heir. So you may speak with complete confidence."

And Blake decided to do so. He had taken an instant liking to this gentleman, despite the fact that he was supposed to be something of a "limb." He seemed crisp of manner, clear cut and decisive in his speech, and Blake liked his eye. Therefore he decided to reveal the exact truth.

"Do you speak English, senor?" he asked in that language.

The other seemed surprised that this dark-skinned visitor, who hailed from Bogota, should speak a foreign language with such perfection, but he was too polite to remark upon it.

"I do," he replied in the same tongue, with scarcely the trace of an accent. "I was at school for four years in England."

Blake waited until the servant who had arrived laid out the drinks and smokes; then, when his host had pushed across some very choice Jamaica cigars, and had poured them a long iced sherbet, Blake went on:

"I am not what I seem, senor. I do not hail from Bogota, and my name is not Ramon Castro. I am an Englishman."

His host smiled.

"I knew you were no Spaniard when you first spoke in English. But why this masquerade, sir? What is the object? And in what way is my niece mixed up in it?"

"Permit me to explain. I shall first give you my proper name. It is Blake—Sexton Blake. I am a criminologist in a private way in London, and—"

"Enough—enough, sir, I pray you. Are you the famous Mr. Sexton Blake of whom I heard and read so much when I was in England?"

"I—I believe there is only one of us," said Blake smilingly.

"Sir, permit me to shake your hand. I am highly honoured. And this"—glancing at Tinker—"is this the assistant of whom I have also heard?"

"It is he."

The exuberant Spaniard must need wring Tinker's hand, too; then he added:

"Your disguise is wonderful. I am a Spaniard, and yet until you used English I never should have suspected a thing. But what are you doing in Santa Marta, Mr. Blake?"

Slowly and carefully Blake told him the whole story—how he had been sent for by Don Fernando to discover evidence against the president if such evidence existed; how he had done so, and then how Don Fernando had got cold feet; of Tinker's capture and of how Carlotta rescued him. This incident wrung some appreciative chuckles from his listener, but he gave eager attention to the rest. When Blake had finished he nodded seriously.

"I can see the whole thing, Mr. Blake. So my brother-in-law lost his nerve! Well, I am not surprised. A fine man, honest as the sun and as straight as a die, but he is getting old. He hasn't been the same since my sister died. He didn't want to enter Don Cristofo's cabinet, but public clamour forced him into it. He disapproves of me. I am too outspoken for his taste, and I love a good horse race, of which Don Fernando stands in horror. Also he thinks I give too much liberty to my niece when she visits me. But that does not worry me. I respect him deeply and know what profound integrity he possesses. I say this so you will understand better, perhaps, some of the things which would influence him. He dreads that this country will go through another period of bloodshed. He would verily give his own life over and over again to prevent it. But it is coming, Mr. Blake, it is coming."

"You mean General Primo de Miguel— the plot to put him in power?"

Guitterez laughed outright.

"It is plain that you do not know what has taken place here in Santa Marta during the last day or two. General Primo de Miguel is no longer a candidate—secret or otherwise."

"Ah! Why has he withdrawn?"

"He didn't withdraw. He was chucked out bag and baggage, as you would say in your country. Or, I should amend that. He was chucked out without either bag or baggage, and with him went one of the worst bullying scoundrels who ever strutted the streets of this town."

"I don't understand, senor. Am I to gather that the revolutionary party have cast him aside?"

"You couldn't understand what I mean. It all happened while you were on your way down from San Jose. But it is rich. The whole town is laughing, and yet not a soul is supposed to be in the know. The position is entirely altered, Mr. Blake. Let me explain. I do not know all the facts, but I have a good many strings out and I hear much— more than most. It all begins with a mulatto woman who came to Santa Marta some months ago."

"You mean the woman known as Marie Galante?"

Guitterez looked surprised.

"How did you know about her?"

"Don Fernando had had letters from Santa Marta; he told me she was here and was mixed up with de Miguel."

"That is correct—or was. She is a devil, that woman—a beautiful devil, I must confess, but she is playing a wicked game down here."

"I know her well. My assistant and I have had dealings with her among the West Indies in the past. We know just what she is and how dangerous. She is beautiful, I grant you."

"Then you will understand what she is capable of doing. Well, it seems that the plot was going ahead smoothly. For there was, and is, a plot, Mr. Blake, and when the storm breaks there is going to be the dickens to pay here in Santa Marta unless —but I shall come to that presently. Well, as you know apparently, General Primo de Miguel, who had been languishing among the islands ever since he was exiled, struck up an acquaintance with this woman Marie Galante. The plot was formed, and she came to Santa Marta to start the ball rolling. She is a wonder, I will say. She has an enormous following on the coast, and every nigger is her slave."

"It is more than just her personality," put in Blake. "Marie Galante is the Voodoo woman of Hayti."

The Spaniard's eyes widened. Even in the dim light which reached them from a swinging lamp some distance away they could see the dilation of his pupils. No one along the Spanish Main or among the islands but knows what Voodoo means and what a sinister thing it is in the lives of the blacks of the whole Caribbean. And Guitterez had heard, of course, of the Mystery Woman of Hayti who was the High Priestess of the terrible rites of the order. Little had he dreamed that the Mystery Woman about whom so many uncanny stories were told was this beautiful fiend who was making her headquarters at a low-class wine shop in the town. He drew a deep breath.

"The Voodoo woman of Hayti," he breathed. "Are you sure?"

"My assistant and I have both seen her at the Voodoo altar," answered Blake after a cautious look round. "I have stood on that altar beside her when she was in the very act of making the blood sacrifice and the deadly fer de lance was writhing at her feet; I have forced her back from that altar by a threat when the great natural ampitheatre in the Haytian jungle was filled with thousands of blacks who would have torn me limb from limb if they had guessed for a moment what was going on. And it is a curious thing, but the very man whom I had followed into that jungle—the man who was working hand-in-glove with Marie Galante at the time—is here in Santa Marta now. I saw him at the Pension Inglesa tonight."

"You mean the big man with the beard?" asked Guitterez in an excited voice.

"That is the man."

"Madre de dios! This opens up much— much that I did not dream of. I shall finish and then we must discuss things, Mr. Blake. What I was telling you has all happened since that man came to Santa Marta. Until then there was no thought of getting rid of General Primo de Miguel. This man with the beard has visited Marie Galante at the wine shop on two or more occasions. The whole truth is not known, but it has come out that last night the general went to the wine shop accompanied by a man of the town known as Julio Bustro—a swaggering bully whom we are well rid of. This man with the beard also visited the wine shop. What took place I cannot tell you, except that a schooner slipped down the river and out to sea without making formal clearance at Dos Hermanos. In that schooner went General Primo de Miguel and Julio Bustro. There is a whisper of a terrible fight at the wine shop, but I do not know just what took place. At any rate, de Miguel and Bustro are out in the Caribbean now, and this man with the beard is master of the woman and cock of the walk.

"To-day the jefe of Santa Marta received an anonymous letter saying that General Primo de Miguel had been in the place for some weeks, but that he had been forcibly deported last night together with his companion, Julio Bustro. The letter also warned the jefe to be on the look-out for their attempt to return. But that is not all. I have told you I have a good many strings out. I hear much, and one thing that has reached me only this evening is about a summons that has gone out to certain members of the revolutionary committee requesting them to attend a secret meeting at the wine shop to-night. What business is to be transacted I don't know unless—well, I have an idea what is afoot."

He broke off there and reached for a fresh cigar. Blake was thinking fast. Rymer and Marie Galante! It certainly looked as if Rymer had again hitched up with the Voodoo woman. But if that was so then where did Mary Trent come into it? Blake did not for a moment believe that Mary Trent would consent to take part in anything which included Marie Galante. He knew that, despite her association with Rymer, she was of a very different type—a girl who would have run dead straight in other circumstances. Both he and Tinker had a sneaking regard for Mary Trent, and knew it was through her love for Rymer that she was what she was. But Mary Trent and Marie Galante—it was unthinkable! What could Rymer be about, Blake was asking himself, to mix the two up together. As a matter of fact Rymer would have given a good deal just then to be able to answer that same question.

Blake began now to attach a much greater importance to Rymer's presence in Santa Marta. It certainly looked, from what Senor Guitterez had just told him, that Rymer was mixed up with Marie Galante in the revolutionary intrigue that had its centre in the mulatto woman. And, for some reason, which was not yet clear, they had decided to get rid of General Primo de Miguel. Then who was to be the candidate? Surely not Rymer. That would be impossible, for only a person who was Santa Martan born could occupy the chair of chief executive of state.

Then whom would they choose? Was that what the secret meeting was called for? And, again, where did Mary Trent come into all this? Who was the young fellow whom Rymer had unquestionably been trying to impress? Just then then Spaniard began to speak again.

"My information is that a new candidate will be presented to the plotters to-night," he said. "And I believe I am one of the few persons in Santa Marta who can point to the person who has been chosen."

"Ah, you know, then?"

"Not for certain; but I have my suspicions. Did you ever hear of Don Ruiz Mendoza, a former dictator-president of Santa Marta?"

"Yes, indeed. I knew him personally."

"Then you knew a real man, despite his morals and his faults. He is dead, worse luck. If he were alive to day he would clean the whole lot of them out and put the country on its feet. Santa Marta would never have been allowed to undergo the shame which has followed the repudiation of the interest on her external debts. Well, Don Ruiz had a son."

"I think I have heard somewhere that he married one of my countrywomen."

"He married a Scotswoman, and, if you will permit me to say so, she must have been a very trying person to live with, from all accounts. At any rate she left Don Ruiz and returned to her own country, taking with her the son who was then but an infant. That son was brought up and educated in your country, Mr. Blake; and that son is in Santa Marta to-day."

"You interest me profoundly, he is a man now, of course."

"A young man of considerable presence, and, were it not for the company he keeps, I should have said of undoubted character. But he travels with the bearded man of whom I have been telling you."

"With Huxton Rymer—why, that must be the red-headed young fellow I saw to-night."

"That is he. He has his mother's hair, but old Don Ruiz's face and figure."

"Good heavens! I see light now. You mean that you think it is he whom Huxton Rymer and Marie Galante intend putting forward as a candidate for the presidency?"

"Huxton Rymer—that is the name. I had heard it, but forgotten. Yes, Mr. Blake, I do mean just that. And let me tell you that if young Don Ruiz Mendoza (his name is the same as his father's) comes out into the open and declares himself as the son of his father he will command an enormous following throughout the country. The people are ripe now for the name of Mendoza to become their slogan. I'll wager, if he does stand forth, as I believe he will, he will sit in the president's chair a week later."

"But—but, sponsored by Huxton Rymer and Marie Galante! Is he mad?"

"Ah! That is what puzzles me. He came to Santa Marta with the man Rymer and the pretty woman who is with him. And he has been with them only ever since. He seems sweet on the pretty woman. And, by the way, Mr. Blake—you who know so much about all those people—tell me what that pretty senorita is doing with the man Rymer? She does not go to the wine shop. She spends her time with young Mendoza visiting the cathedral and other old buildings. I do not understand her. She seems a nice person, and yet she is something more than just a friend to him. You see, I hear much, as I said."

Blake explained something of what he knew the relationship to be between Rymer and Mary Trent. But he had to confess that he was utterly at sea to understand what she could be doing in Santa Marta if Rymer was mixed up with Marie Galante.

"I am positive she cannot know of his past connection with the Voodoo woman," he said, when he had ended the relation. "I know her quite well. She is a girl who is deeply devoted to Rymer, and she has been his helpmeet in many a swindle. But she is different from Marie Galante. I do not understand it at all. I am wondering if Rymer came to Santa Marta at the invitation of Marie Galante or whether—"

Suddenly he brought the palm of his hand softly against his thigh.

"An idea has come to me, senor. Listen. You say that it is only since Huxton Rymer came to Santa Marta that the action was taken to got rid of General Primo de Miguel."

"That is so. He went last night."

"And Rymer has only been here for about three days. You say that young Mendoza arrived with him?"

"Yes. I have ascertained that they came by the same ship. Mind you, I fancy I am about the only person outside that immediate circle who suspects this young man is the son of old Ruiz Mendoza, the dictator."

"Yes. Well, supposing there was still another plot afoot to make a bid for the presidency? What if Huxton Rymer had that in his mind before he came to Santa Marta? How would it appear to you if you considered it from that angle—that somewhere he had picked up young Mendoza, and, after learning his history, had realised the possibilities? I can assure you that Rymer could so conduct himself that Mendoza would never guess he was a crook. And he would be most ably supported by Mary Trent. Then let us say that after reaching Santa Marta he found Marie Galante here— stumbled on another intrigue? Wouldn't it strengthen his hand if he could swing her party over to his? And I have reason to know that Marie Gallante would have gone a long way in the past for Huxton Rymer. I am presuming she would still do so. What do you think of that theory?"

Senor Guitterez thought so well of it that he was fairly hopping up and down in his chair with excitement. As soon as Blake finished speaking he burst out:

"That is why you are a great detective. Your mind goes out at once to essentials. You have struck it, Mr. Blake, you have struck it— I am sure. That explains the whole thing. So what now?"

Blake shrugged.

"I don't know. I'd give a lot to attend that secret meeting to-night, but I suppose that is out of the question."

"It is too late to arrange it now; but tomorrow I shall have a full report of what takes place. I have a string out there as well. It pays me in my business to know these things."

Blake excused himself, and, rising, took to walking up and down the length of the patio. He was thinking over the theory which had come to him so suddenly, and from that he went on to consider in detail each human factor who loomed as a major item in the puzzle. Over young Mendoza he mulled for a considerable time; then, suddenly he wheeled and returned to where his host and Tinker were sitting.

"Senor," he said quickly, "before we left San Jose your niece extracted a promise from me."

"Yes; that is like her. What was the promise, Mr. Blake?"

"That if there was any way at all in which I thought she could be of assistance I should telegraph for her to come down."

"Well?"

"I have an idea working in my mind in which she may be able to help. Would you send a telegram to her, senor, and ask her to come down at once to pay you a visit? She will understand."

"You are not going to let her mix up in this business?"

"Not in any way that can possibly hurt her; I pledge you my word on that. I cannot say more now. I shall unfold my plans just as soon as I can work them out."

"Very well, Mr. Blake, I shall do as you ask. I shall get a telegram off through Government channels so that it will go tonight. She should be able to catch the train from San Jose to-morrow morning, which would bring her here the evening of the day after."

"Thank you, senor. I shaft explain, I hope, to-morrow. But first I want to study things at the hotel. We shall return now."

"You and your assistant will take breakfast with me to-morrow?" remarked the Spaniard as he rose. (Breakfast in Santa Marta was lunch and breakfast combined, and took place at eleven o'clock.)

"With pleasure."

"I may have news about to-night's meeting to give you."

"I hope so. Every grain will help now."

And so they took their departure. As soon as they were in the street Tinker wanted to know why Blake was sending for Carlotta, but all his master would reply was:

"I hardly know myself yet, young 'un. Wait and see. I'll tell you as soon as I see if there is a chance to pull off a scheme that is in my mind."

More than that Tinker could not get out of him.

CHAPTER 13. "Hell hath no fury like a woman scorned—"

ALTHOUGH his plans to put young Mendoza in the presidential chair of Santa Marta appeared to be moving smoothly enough, Huxton Rymer was being more and more harassed by the multiplication of complications arising in his private affairs.

Until the secret meeting at the wine shop on the night following the forcible expulsion of General Primo de Miguel from the country he had been able, by a certain degree of finesse and evasiveness, to keep from Mary Trent the extent of his association with Marie Galante. But, following that meeting, when Ruiz Mendoza had been presented to the revolutionists as their candidate and had been accepted with enthusiastic acclaim, Mary had got to know about the mulatto woman.

It was Mendoza who told her, and he did so in all innocence that Rymer would have preferred him to remain mute on that subject. But there had been, too, a little waning of eagerness on the part of Mendoza, despite the enthusiasm displayed by his supporters.

There seemed to him to be something not altogether in keeping with his dignity as president-to-be in this hole and corner conference in a dingy wine shop. And, certainly, some of those present had been of the rag-tag and bobtail of the town. Nor had he been favourably impressed by the intensely exotic mulatto woman who seemed, aside from his own sponsor, to dominate the proceedings.

For the first time he discovered that he would owe much to her if he gained the chair, and he did not like the feeling. Which goes to show that not only did young Mendoza possess scruples which were beginning to assert themselves, but he also was acquiring consciousness of dignity that was threatening to raise difficulties for Rymer unless he could keep him in hand. So far he had been able to do so because the young man liked him and felt that he owed everything to him—because, too, Mary wielded a tremendous influence over him.

But he was discovering that while he liked her immensely, his feeling was not the wild love he had thought it to be. In that was proof of what Mary had said to Rymer when they were still on board ship, and it is altogether probable that it was partially due to her gentle, sisterly attitude when they were alone that realisation came to Mendoza.

100

He still sought her out at every opportunity and told her all his thoughts. Hence it was that he dwelt at some length of the mulatto woman who had been present at the secret meeting, and it had not taken Mary long to discover that he disliked her and would be better pleased if she were not mixed up in the business.

Now Mary had heard of Marie Galante before. She knew that the mulatto woman had been something in Rymer's past, but she had never hinted this knowledge to Rymer. Mary was a wise little girl, and believed in always keeping a card back if possible. It came to her then, as something of an unpleasant shock to learn that she was in intimate association with Rymer in these matters.

Why hadn't he told her about the other? From the remarks let drop by Mendoza it was plain to her that Rymer had been seeing the mulatto woman ever since he came to Santa Marta. And yet he had not breathed a word to her. Had he, she asked herself jealously, known all the time that Marie Galante was in Santa Marta? Had he heard from her when he was in England; and was that what had started him off to the Caribbean? Had he brought her along only because he could not think up a reasonable excuse for leaving her behind? Was he still keen on this jungle cat? And was he at heart tired of her?

She was miserable and jealous; and all that afternoon she remained in her room, pleading a headache. She wanted to think. If Rymer was playing a double game then she knew what she would do. But, on the other hand, she wasn't going to stand meekly by while this sleeky cat from Hayti took him away from her, as if she could bring him to heel by a snap of her fingers.

A slow anger began to rise in her at the thought, and by the time she appeared at dinner it would have taken a keener eye than Rymer's to guess that anything was wrong. Mary was biding her time.

There was another thing which was occupying Rymer's mind, and that may be why he did not scrutinise her too closely or wonder if her headache had been genuine. This had to do with the presence at dinner the previous evening of a tall Spaniard and a dark-skinned youth who had sat on the other side of the patio.

Mary had watched them, and during the meal had leant across to whisper to him that there was something about the profile of the man that reminded her of Sexton Blake. Rymer had not turned to look then, and when he had taken occasion to do so, he had found them gone. A little later as he and his party had entered the lobby, he had caught a glimpse of the pair, but did not get a chance to scrutinise their features.

He knew Mary would not make the remark idly, and yet he could hardly believe that Sexton Blake and Tinker were in Santa Marta. He took early opportunity to look at the register, and there he saw that two visitors had arrived the night before—one Ramon Castro and friend. Their address was given as in the Caille Bolivar at Bogota, Colombia, and, by discreet inquiries, Rymer found that they had come down from San Jose by river steamer. It didn't look as if it could be Blake and Tinker, and yet—

Since that he had not caught a glimpse of them. He was able to ascertain that they were still staying at the hotel, although they were out from early morning until late at night. As a matter of fact, the Senor Guittorez had insisted on them making his residence their headquarters, and while Blake would not consent to move there entirely (for he wanted to keep on their rooms at the Pension Inglesa so as to be able to go there at any hour of the day or night as developments might suggest) they did take all their rneals there and spent most of their time in the lovely patio. Hence Rymer, who was also abroad a good deal, failed to catch another sight of them.

This was the position of things on the night after the secret meeting at the wine shop; and when, as they were finishing dinner, he said that he should have to go out again that evening, Mary did not raise any question. But she did ask if Ruiz would be going too. Rymer had not intended asking for him, for there was a good deal he wanted to talk over privately with Marie Galante, and he was annoyed at Mary raising the question.

But when Mendoza said that if it was on the business in which they were interested he should like to come, Rymer could not very well refuse to take him. So it was that the two started out together, and if Rymer was not too enthusiastic over having Mendoza as his companion, Marie Galante was furious that he did not come alone.

Luckily for Rymer there were several customers in the wine shop that evening. While Marie Galante could clear the place —and would have done so quickly enough if it had suited her purpose—when necessary, she could not always retain it simply for the meetings of the revolutionary committee. That would cause gossip and attract the unwelcome attention of the police.

But she had kept the back room clear, and there she had expected to have a long to tête-à-tête with Rymer, during which she intended to settle once and for all just where she stood.

Rymer should have been grateful for Mendoza's presence, for he was far from anxious to have the mulatto woman bring things to a head. If she learned the truth about Mary she was quite capable of wrecking the whole plot, and he knew it.

The evening could not be said to have passed pleasantly. Marie Galante's eyes were smouldering with a fire that threatened to burst out at any moment, and it was plain to Rymer that young Mendoza was not only uncomfortable in the woman's presence, but disliked her as well.

Marie Galante returned his aversion. Between the two, Rymer was glad when some of the other members of the revolutionary party came in and the talk could be switched. Nothing in the shape of really secret plans could be discussed; nor was it necessary.

The propaganda was already at work among the people. It had been decided the night before that a week should be devoted to this, and at the end of that time things would be ripe to strike. A final meeting a few days hence was to decide the exact moment when the rising should take place and Ruiz Mendoza stand out before the people as their leader.

The whole thing was to be done on a most spectacular plan, and at the same moment another rising would take place in San Jose. They expected to sweep into power in both places within a few hours, and with the capital as well as the chief port in their hands, the whole country would be theirs. It was a good plan, and there seemed no reason why it shouldn't be a success.

Rymer was only too glad to find an excuse to get away. The future president could not be expected to spend too much time in such a place, despite the fact that it was his temporary headquarters, so to say. Nor could he be allowed to walk back alone. The gang which was collected there were out for just one thing, pickings; but, at the same time, there was a dignity about young Ruiz Mendoza that commanded their respect, and they were not forgetful of the fact that he was the son of the great dictator, Ruiz Mendoza. The only person to whom these things didn't matter a straw was Marie Galante.

However, even she was not going to burst out before others; so, while her lips smiled her eyes spoke volumes to Rymer when he passed out. He breathed easier when he was in the street, but no sooner were they well away from the place than his companion spoke of the mulatto woman.

"Do you know, Professor Butterfield, I should have been better pleased if we could have got along without that woman. I do not like her, and I am sure she does not like me."

"I agree that it would have been better; but what would you, Ruiz? When we arrived here I found that a strong revolutionary plot was already in progress. If it had been allowed to proceed we should not have stood a chance. We might have wrecked their plans, and they would have certainly wrecked ours. In the mix-up the Gouffra party would have remained in power. The only thing to do was to blend their organisation with our aims, and, if you will pardon me for speaking of my own part, I think I managed rather well in doing so. I disposed of General Primo de Miguel in summary fashion. Nothing else would have served. There could be no compromise. And; moreover, that woman carries with her every single black on the coast. They are not a desirable class in Santa Marta; but, if you march to the president's chair, Ruiz, you must have no preference for classes or creeds."

The little speech contained some expression of ideals worthy of a better man than Rymer.

Mendoza sighed.

"Of course you are right, professor. Please do not think I am finding fault. I am not. Nor am I ungrateful. I owe everything to you, and I shall always be your debtor. It just struck me that it would be better if we could have had—well, a little better element in with us."

"When we strike our blow every element will be with us," Rymer assured him. "You are getting nervy, Ruiz. I do not know that it wouldn't be better to advance the date. There is no real reason why we should give a whole week to the propaganda. Everything is ready up in San Jose. To-morrow I shall go into matters, and see if it isn't possible for us to fix the rising for say, three nights hence. Believe me, my boy, everything I am doing is for your best interests."

"Oh, I know that, sir. You and Miss Trent have been wonderful to me. When I am president you will not find me forgetful."

Rymer would take good care that he wasn't, but he only said:

"Time enough for that, my boy—time enough for that!"

The next morning Rymer decided to go to the wine shop and

have it out with Marie Galante. He knew things were reaching a crisis, and for his own sake he was anxious enough to have the rising fixed for three nights hence instead of a week. With all the details to attend to, the comings and goings there would be, the mulatto woman wouldn't have any excuse for complaining that he was trying to avoid her.

And after it was over—well, he had dished old de Miguel, and, as the president's right-hand counsellor, he could soon get rid of the woman, too. Which goes to show that Rymer was honestly trying to play the game with Mary Trent. But he found that Mary had something to say to him that morning which couldn't wait.

She had had another talk with Ruiz, and had learned enough about the previous evening to make her so uneasy that she could not wait any longer without putting matters to the test. Mary was capable of as much depth of feeling as Marie Galante, only she was of a different race, and wouldn't show it in the same way.

Rymer suggested that they leave the talk until the afternoon. But Mary shook her head, and insisted gently that they should have it then. Poor Rymer could not refuse. He was getting savage, and was anathematising all women as he walked with her to the public gardens, which lie just beyond the cathedral. If he had known that a negro lad had watched them emerge from the hotel, and was trailing them, he would have felt a deal more savage.

He had a hunch that Mary had something to say about Marie Galante. It had, of course, been impossible for him to tell Mendoza not to mention the mulatto woman to Mary. Such a request would at once have caused the young fellow to wonder why his friend, Professor Butterfield, should wish to conceal the fact that the woman was mixed up in the plotting. He thought that Rymer had accepted her as a necessary evil, knowing nothing about the "professor" being Huxton Rymer, the notorious adventurer.

And, of course, Marie Galante was nothing but a name to him. In fact, Rymer had hoped that Mendoza had not caught her name; but he was soon to be enlightened, for, when Mary had led him to a secluded bench in the gardens, she turned to him, and, laying one hand on his knee, said:

"Why didn't you tell me about Marie Galante?"

"Er—how—what do you mean, Mary?"

"Don't hedge, old boy. Let us have things quite frank between us.

Ruiz has told me. He didn't know, of course, that it meant anything, and I will confess that I pumped him without his knowing it. You see, I know that you had something to do with her in the past. I have never mentioned it, because it would only revive things that I thought were better left alone. But she is here in this town now; she is taking a leading part in the plotting, and you are with her a good deal. Just where do I stand in this?

"You know, old boy, that you can't have your cake and eat it, and—and no matter how much I care for you, I will not have another woman taking a part in your life. I am ready to make arrangements to leave Santa Marta at once. There is a ship clearing from Dos Hermanos to-morrow; but I am not going without giving you a chance to tell me just where I stand. The fact that you have said nothing proves that you wanted to conceal it."

Rymer shifted uncomfortably. She was dead right, and he knew it. How could he make her believe that she was the only woman he cared a straw for? What would she say if she knew that he had had Marie Galante in his arms, and had felt her burning lips on his since he had been in Santa Marta? It was the very dickens of a mess, the only thing to do was to tell the truth as far as he dared, and leave the decision in Mary's hands. So he went at it.

She listened while he told her how he had found the mulatto woman at the wine shop when he went to pick up what information he could; explained why it had been necessary to join forces with her; and gave her his word that as soon as the whole business was over he would break with her utterly; that she and she only held his regard; and so on.

Mary listened in silence. She was hearing what she wanted to hear. But there was one question she still had to put, and on Rymer's answer to that depended everything. When he was done she asked it.

"Tell me, and tell me truly," she said, in a low tone, twisting her hands together, "have you taken that woman's caresses since you have been here?"

Neither she nor Rymer realised how tense were their altitudes just then. They were too absorbed in what they were saying.

He did not know how to answer the question. He was going to play for time. But it was not to be necessary; he would never have to answer it. For, as he bent towards Mary, some moving bushes just opposite them caught his eye, and he stiffened suddenly as the leaves parted, and he found himself gazing straight into the furious, blazing eyes of Marie Galante.

Mary did not see the mulatto woman. She was waiting for Rymer to speak. Then she felt him stiffen, and, after that, she only knew that for some reason he uttered an oath and threw himself in front of her. Out of the bushes had come a glittering knife, hurled by the insane strength of a jungle creature who was in a paroxysm of terrible jealousy. Straight as perfect aiming could send it was that dagger speeding for Mary Trent's heart when Rymer threw himself in front of her.

Something struck him, then Mary struggled up with a cry of horrified alarm as Rymer slid to the ground and rolled over, a crimson stain spreading rapidly through the white shoulder of his linen coat.

CHAPTER 14.   Carlotta Arrives, and Has a Secret Talk with Blake—Ruiz Mendoza Becomes Demoralised, and Has His Eyes Opened.

BLAKE, Tinker and Senor Guitterez all went to the jetty to meet Carlotta. That afternoon Blake had instructed Tinker to remove his disguise. He did the same, feeling a lot cleaner and fresher when he had got rid of the fringe of a beard which he had grown. Since the previous night they had been lying low. They had slept at the hotel as usual, but they had got away very early in the morning, taking coffee with Guitterez.

Blake desired to keep out of Rymer's way until he had a chance to put to the test the plan that he was forming in his mind. But he did not take the trouble to find out under what name Rymer was travelling, and when he discovered it was the nome de guerre he had used on several former occasions, he began to suspect that Ruiz Mendoza could not know the identity of his companions.

They heard nothing of what had happened in the gardens during the morning until just before they were starting out to meet Carlotta. Then a man arrived to see Senor Guitterez, and when their host rejoined them it was to tell them this bit of news. Blake was puzzled. Guitterez did not seem to have learned many details. The whole affair was wrapped in mystery, but it seemed that Rymer had started out for a walk with Mary Trent and that about an hour later they had returned to the hotel in a cab—the man appearing very weak from a wound which had stained his white coat crimson.

A doctor had been sent for, and it was said at the hotel that the wound was a painful gash in the shoulder, but not dangerous. So much for that; but, naturally, Blake was not a little intrigued to know what had happened. He wasn't so far out of the truth when he wondered if it had had anything to do with a clash between Mary Trent and Marie Galante.

Carlotta's boat came in almost up to time —for a wonder. She was puzzled but pleased to see Blake and Tinker as themselves, and the greeting between her and her uncle was very warm, for they were great chums. Tinker blushed when he caught the duenna's eye, but that elderly soul ignored him with the exception of a frigid little bow in response to his salute. The good soul felt, now that the episode was past, that, she had lost something of dignity through taking part in such a wild escapade.

They drove back to the Guitterez mansion at once, and, when Carlotta and the duenna had taken some refreshment, Blake lost no time in getting the girl alone and telling her what was in his mind. As he spoke, her lovely eyes filled first with a spirit of mischief, and she could not help breaking into little thrills of enjoyment from time to time. But before he had finished she was sober enough, for a doubt had come into her mind.

"Of course I will do what you suggest, Mr. Blake. I will do anything for my country. But, suppose—suppose there are any complications? What if he does not respond as you think he will?"

"He could not fail to do so and be human, senorita," returned Blake gallantly, but none the less genuinely. For she was certainly looking very lovely.

Her eyes flashed into his for a moment, and even Blake, old stager though he was, felt a sudden thrill shoot through him. She could play the very dickens with any man if she chose.

"And then—what if he should take it seriously?" she went on.

"Or you?" he added.

She nodded and breathed: "Yes."

Blake rubbed his chin thoughtfully. He had been hoping she would not raise this point. Finally he looked at her with that winning smile which could be very attractive when he chose.

"That is one of the fortunes of war, senorita. Perhaps, before you finish, you might not want it ended."

She blushed gloriously and rose.

"You are too direct, Mr. Blake. But I shall do what you ask. You can depend on me to get my full battery in action."

"Then I haven't a doubt of the outcome," he answered before she flitted away.

Still Blake kept mum about his plans, he had arranged that the four of them— Carlotta, Guitterez, Tinker and himself, should dine at the hotel, and then they should see what they should see. The duenna was to be left behind, as Guitterez would be sufficient chaperone for his neice. In those countries they are great sticklers about girls going about unchaperoned.

Carlotta was a vision of perfectly adorable loveliness when she at last joined them in the patio. The three males paid her a prompt and deep tribute as they bowed and, whatever misgivings Carlotta may have had, whatever qualms may have assailed her, she had put them away now and was out to bring her full battery into action as she had promised Blake.

They were all in the best of humours as they entered Guitterez's big saloon car and drove to the Pension Inglesa. Blake had taken trouble the night before to reserve a large corner table in the patio, and he had chosen it with an eye to the position of the one occupied by Rymer and his party.

He had been calculating as part of his plans that Rymer would be present during the meal, but if he did not show up he would put his plans into effect some other way. It wasn't necessary for what he had in mind that Rymer should be there, but it was essential that Ruiz Mendoza should be present; and it would suit Blake better if Mary Trent were there.

He arranged his party so that Carlotta must face the other table, and then as he seated himself he raised his eyes. He smiled inwardly as he saw, that despite his wound, Rymer had come down. One side of his coat was hanging loosely, and his left arm was in a sling; his face was pale enough to show that the wound, however it had been caused, was no joke.

Blake did not bow, for Rymer had not caught his eye. The moment he was waiting for had not yet arrived. But, when he shot a glance at young Mendoza, who was full face to Carlotta, he saw that his plan was going to work out more speedily and with a greater vengeance than he had dreamed. For now it may be said that Blake had decided to use permissible lure to win Ruiz Mendoza away from the company he was keeping.

That was but the first step in the campaign which he was working out, and he figured that if Carlotta could be brought in to help, she would do the trick quicker than it could be accomplished in any other way.

And she was doing it! From the moment his eyes had fallen on the lovely vision at the next table, Ruiz Mendoza had fallen in love head over heels. He had frozen in his seat with sheer wonder at the loveliness of the girl, and for the better part of a minute he forgot his manners enough to stare at her as if she were a ghost.

Mary Trent, who had seen, brought him back to the present with a word, and from that on he was studiously attentive to her, Rymer had missed this by-play and Mary did not signal anything to him yet.

She was watching and waiting, for her quick intuition had seen ahead to just what this might lead if Ruiz managed to get to know this vision who had come in with Blake, Tinker and another man.

Rymer had, of course, seen Blake and Tinker, but he had ignored them. Blake was willing that this should be so until he was ready to take the next step. He wanted to give Carlotta's "medicine" time to get in its work well and, judging from appearances, young Mendoza would be gibbering before long if something didn't bring him out of the trance he was in.

It was as bad a case of, literally, love at first sight as Blake had ever seen, and his mind reverted to Carlotta's objections. She had foreseen this possibility. And now Blake was asking himself what she was thinking of Mendoza.

He was a good-looking, well set up young fellow whose face was full of earnestness and whose eyes were the mirrors of a lofty mind. Would Carlotta feel drawn to him in the same way? If so, then Blake would have to keep a steady hand on the helm.

It was when the meal was drawing to a close that the moment came for which Blake had been waiting. With a quick, significant look at Carlotta he rose and walked deliberately to the other table.

Pausing so that he was facing Mary Trent, he bowed:

"How do you do, Miss Trent?" he said easily "I thought I could not be mistaken. And you, Professor Butterfield, how are you? Are you and Miss Trent travelling for pleasure, or are you here on some scientific mission?"

Mary smiled coolly and put out her hand.

After a moment's hesitation Rymer forced a smile, but all the time he was thinking:

"Now, what the dickens does this mean? Why is he bolstering up our bluff? Why didn't he call me by my right name and be done with it. He's playing some deep game, that is certain."

Ruiz Mendoza saw none of this tension.

Instead he was seraphically delighted that someone from Carlotta's table knew his friends, for that meant an introduction. And, as a matter of fact, Mary was forced to present him to Blake a moment later.

"She did not name him as "Sexton Blake," but just called him Mr. Blake and let it go at that. Then Blake fired his next shot.

"My host, Senor Jose Guitterez, wishes me to invite you all to join him at coffee at his house. We are so few here and when he understood that I knew you he made the suggestion. It would give him great pleasure."

Rymer and Mary were more puzzled than ever. Why was Blake seeking their company? Rymer knew of Jose Guitterez well enough—knew of him as the wealthiest citizen of Santa Marta and a man of a good deal of mystery. Indeed, it had been mooted that he should be approached to join the revolutionary cabinet, but it had been vetoed because his brother-in-law was a member of the present government.

But what game was Blake playing? They got nothing from those cool grey eyes but subtle mockery. And, unless young Mendoza was to become suspicious, how could they refuse. It would be easy enough for Rymer to plead that he was not well enough and, of course, Mary could say that she could not leave him. But that would Mendoza going round alone, and could not risk letting him loose when Sexton Blake was round. He didn't know what to say, but Mary came to the rescue in just the right way.

"My uncle is not well enough—I am sorry," she said, looking Blake so straight in the eye that he had to admire her nerve. "But Senor Mendoza would like to go, I am sure, and I shall be happy to come with him."

"That will be delightful; I trust you not seriously indisposed, Professor. I have noticed that you carry your arm in a sling."

Rymer could not resist glaring at him. He was wondering if Blake knew how he got the wound.

"It is nothing much," he said carelessly, "an accident." Then he smiled at Mendoza. "You and Miss Trent go by all means, Ruiz."

And so it was arranged. As soon as dinner was over the two parties came together. Blake made the introductions, and it must be confessed that Tinker grinned frankly when he was presented to Mary Trent. The lad had a warm spot in his heart for Mary despite her association with Rymer. It was decided that the two girls, with Ruiz and Tinker, should drive on in the car, while Blake and Guitterez were to walk. So, when the car had gone off, they talked for a few minutes with Rymer and then started.

As they passed out Rymer's gaze met Blake's for just a moment, but Blake's countenance was as blank as a wall. Rymer returned to the patio more puzzled than ever, and after a few seconds thought, he made up his mind he would take the opportunity to go to the wine shop and see Marie Galante. A show-down was certainly in order after the events of the morning.

Senor Guitterez had created an ideal "mise en scene" for Blake's plan. While they were at the hotel servants had strung coloured paper lanterns through the patio and all the fountains had been turned on. In that mass of green and scented blooms it was as romantic a setting as one could conceive, and when, after they had taken coffee and were sitting talking idly— Guitterez and Blake devoting themselves to Mary Trent—it was a very simple matter for Carlotta to rise and wander away through the gloom with Ruiz Mendoza keeping close to her.

Mary Trent gave one look at Blake— a look of mingled anger and unwilling admiration. She knew now, as well as if he had told her everything beforehand, just what he had been aiming at, and she was furious that she could not do a single thing to prevent it. To have done so would have been to play straight into Blake's power—not that he didn't hold all the cards in that hand as it was.

But a word from him would have unveiled Rymer, and Mary knew that Blake was quite capable of exposing the adventurer if he thought it best to do so. She was forced to sit and smile and talk nothings while she was seething with fury inwardly. And all the time Blake smiled with a sardonic look in his eye.

When Carlotta and Ruiz finally sauntered back at the end of half an hour Blake had only to take one look at the young man to see that he had been routed "horse and foot." He was as near the state of babbling idiocy of emotion as love can bring an ordinary, well-balanced person.

Blake was satisfied that beyond there in the scented dusk he had unburdened himself to Carlotta as fully as she would permit. He had been bowled over more desperately than Blake had calculated on, and it was as plain as a pikestaff that this was no fleeting infatuation. His eyes were full of an awesome adoration that only comes to a man once in a life time. It would go hard with him if he did not win Carlotta.

As for that vision of loveliness, her dark eyes were shining like stars. She had drawn a canary silk mantilla tightly about her and stood there in the soft light, vibrant with youth and life—every tender curve of her lovely body outlined against the soft light.

Mendoza acted as if he had been drugged. When Mary suggested that they should return he assented readily enough, but he could not tear his eyes away from Carlotta, and, as he bent over her hand, Blake heard him plead that he might see her early on the morrow. She gave her assent, and he went off with Mary prepared to spend the night dreaming of this wonderful creature who had dropped from heaven.

As soon as they were gone Carlotta smiled a little wearily at Blake. She said good-night to her uncle, and Tinker and Blake knew he had meant to walk across to the other side of the patio with her. When they were out of sight of the others she stopped and pressed her hands against his broad chest.

"I feel wicked and mean," she almost sobbed. "He's not a schemer, Mr. Blake; he has the finest ideals. He is splendid. What shall I do?"

Blake put one hand over hers.

"Why do you feel mean?" he asked gently. "Do you think I should have exposed you to such a thing as this unless I had convinced myself that he was all right? I believe he is a most upright young fellow. And if that is so, don't you want to take him away from people who can only do him harm?"

"Yes, but—"

"You have seen that he has fallen desperately in love with you. You regard him therefore with different eyes. Have no fear, little girl, he will come to no harm through me or any of the plans I may lay."

"Oh, I know that—I know it. Mr. Blake! But it made me want to tell him the truth. He thinks the man he is with is honest and straight. And he is very fond of Miss Trent."

Blake could not help smiling. There was just a hint of jealousy in her last words. It told him more than anything that Carlotta had not escaped unscathed and, gazing down at her, he knew it would go very hard with her if she chose wrongly.

"Trust me, little girl," he said quietly. "You will see that everything will come right."

She laid her cheek against his hand, then she flitted away through the gloom. Blake waited until she disappeared, then he walked slowly back to the others, murmuring as he went:

"I'm blessed but it does look as if I were going to be responsible for a match out of all this. Carlotta—that girl would be just the wife for him if he did become president. And, after all, why shouldn't he?"

But Blake was not the only one to spring a surprise that night. As soon as he had finished relating the success of the plan which Carlotta had carried out. Guitterez nodded his head in satisfaction.

"Good! Carlotta, bless her, has accomplished more in one evening than I had expected would be done in several days. I could see that young Mendoza was hit hard. That makes it possible for me to unfold a little secret of my own."

He paused in order to light a fresh cigar, and then went on:

"You and this man Rymer and the mulatto woman and all the rest are not alone in planning revolutions. I, myself, have been indulging for a long time past. There is a small coterie of us here in Santa Marla with plenty of money behind us, and with the jefo and commandant of the garrison ready to throw their weight with us when we give the word." Blake gave a low exclamation of surprise, but did not interrupt. "We have not acted because we were not ready. We lacked the proper candidate. If my brother-in-law would have stepped forward we should have carried him in easily. But as you know he jibbed at the responsibility at his age. We have been ready and waiting to join any party that had an honest man to run. We are determined that Cristofo Gouffra shall not steal any more from this country. But we could not endorse old Primo de Miguel, who is a scoundrel. That is why we have been lying low, watching the move of every other party. That is why I was so interested to see what you would make of it all.

"And you have pulled the chestnuts out of the fire in a most masterly manner, if you will permit me to say so. You have given us just the candidate we need. You have picked him out right from under the noses of those who think he is their meek tool in the only way it could have been done. He is the access of strength we needed—the rallying point to which all classes and creeds will rush. Therefore I say—why wait before we spring the trap? Why let these poor fools, who think Ruiz Mendoza will run with them, spoil everything? Why not strike now—to-night?"

Blake drew a deep breath.

"Senor, you amaze me. If what you say is true then—why not? I have no doubt that Ruiz Mendoza will run with us. But only one person can convince him—can make him act as quickly as is necessary."

"You mean Carlotta?"

"Yes. And if she does bring him over to us you know what he

will think—what he must think."

"I know that. I have been considering it all the evening."

"And you would be prepared for that?"

"Yes. Carlotta has taken to him as well. With that girl as his wife I should know that this poor country would have a good president."

"I agree, most emphatically. In that case, senor, I am with you."

"This very night?"

"This very night."

"Your hands—both of you."

And thus they pledged themselves to the great adventure.

They went into plans at once. If they acted swiftly they could strike by dawn. There was Ruiz Mendoza to get hold of without Rymer knowing. Carlotta would convince him that he must come in with them. She would know how to overcome his scruples about letting down Rymer and Mary Trent. They had no fear there.

Then there was the jefo and the commandant to be warned; Guitterez's friends to be told that the hour had struck. Every light in Santa Marta must come on as soon as a gun was fired at the garrison; the commandant must have his troops ready to sweep the streets immediately after. Mendoza must be held where he could be rushed to the steps of the cathedral to be shown to the people and make his call to them. A large crowd must be kept in readiness to rush up and down the main thoroughfares crying the name— Ruiz Mendoza. It would be the rallying cry.

These and half a hundred other details they went through swiftly, and they had reached the point where they were just about to start the ball rolling, when a peon came rushing across the patio followed by a woman who seemed to be on the point of collapse. Blake turned his head and jumped to his feet just in time to catch Mary Trent in his arms.

CHAPTER 15.   What the Night of Drama Brought to Santa Marta and Those Who Took Part in the Wild Play of Passion That Was Let Loose.

HE eased her into a chair and bent over her.

"What is it—what has upset you so?"

"It is he—he is in that place, and I don't know what is happening— something terrible—fighting, and he is wounded."

"You mean Rymer."

"Yes—yes. I went there to find him. I could hear a terrible fight. You must do something—it is your fault that he is there."

Blake couldn't quite follow her woman's logic that it was his fault that Rymer was in trouble, but he didn't stress that point then. He could see that she was in deep distress, and that was enough for Sexton Blake.

"Calm yourself, Miss Trent," he said quietly. "I shall go at once, I promise you. But where is he?"

"At the wine shop!"

"You mean where Marie Galante is?"

"Yes," she answered chokingly.

"And you have been there? Are you sure he is in trouble?"

"Oh! Listen."

Swiftly she told him what had happened in the gardens in the morning; then she explained that Rymer had confessed it was Marie Galante who had thrown the knife. She thought he must have gone there after she and Mendoza had come round to take coffee. At any rate, on getting back to the hotel she had found him missing and had gone in search of him, fearing that he would not be safe. The knife throwing had frightened her.

"And Mendoza?"

"He is at the hotel."

"He does not know?"

"No; I went out after he had gone to his room."

"Very well; now listen. I am going to that wine shop. I know where it is, and I shall not return without Rymer. I promise you that. Now, you stay here and get calm. Everything will be all right." Then he hurried across to Guitterez who had been standing, listening in amazement and not knowing what to do.

"I'll go and get him," said Blake quickly. "Will you go ahead

117

with everything, just as we planned? I shall join you as soon as possible, but while I am at the wine shop I can smash that business to pieces. It will be as well."

"Then you mustn't go alone. That woman has a rotten gang there. I'll get through at once to the commandant and have him send a flying squad along to help."

"That will be better. But I shall start now. You will go ahead? Mendoza is at the hotel and knows nothing."

"I shall spring the trap the moment you are gone."

Blake beckoned to Tinker.

"Come on, young 'un."

Tinker, who had only been waiting the word, paused just long enough to whisper an assurance to Mary Trent. He was not forgetting what she had done for him some time before in Morocco, at no little risk to herself; and it hurt him to see her in such distress.

They raced across the patio towards the gates. Just before they reached them, Blake caught a glimpse of a white figure hastening down the stairs. He knew it was Carlotta who must have been roused by the commotion, and was coming to see what was wrong. It was a good thing, for she could do more for Mary Trent than anyone else; and, incidentally, she would be on hand to play her part with Mendoza.

"What do you think has happened?" panted Tinker as they raced along.

"It's that mulatto," jerked Blake. "She has been crazy about Rymer for years, he must have gone there to see her, and I suppose there has been an unholy row about Mary Trent. I shouldn't be surprised if the woman has gone off the deep end completely, and has tried to force him, in some way, to leave with her. If she ever gets Rymer back into those Hatian jungles it will be his finish."

As a matter of fact, Blake had hit it just about right. Rymer had gone to have a settlement, and a terrible scene had followed. But what Rymer did not know —nor Blake—was that Marie Galante had her own schooner in waiting among the mangroves across the river. That afternoon, consumed by an awful flame of jealousy, she had determined to throw everything to the winds and leave Santa Marta. But Rymer was to go with her. She knew the big adventurer would refuse, and she had prepared for that.

Rymer had put up a terrific fight against a score of blacks who had rushed up from the jetty at a signal from Marie Galante.

It was that fight which Mary had heard when she went to look for him. But Rymer had been overpowered by numbers, and even as Blake and Tinker raced towards the spot, Marie Galante was feverishly preparing to leave.

They found the wine shop in seeming darkness, and could hear nothing when they reached it. But that did not stop them. Together they drove bodily through the locked outer door and raced on through into the back room where a smoky oil lamp still swung from the ceiling. On the floor lay three blacks, two dead, and one badly wounded.

That was enough for Blake. He knew all about the jetty at the back, and somehow he sensed what the plan was. He led the way to the door which gave on to the steps, and the moment they had dragged it open they saw what was going on.

A schooner lay at the jetty, ready to leave, as they knew. A naked flare was burning, and this lit up the hurrying forms of negroes who were throwing bundles over the rail. Standing on the dock, directing them and looking like some devilishly alluring spirit of evil from the black heart of the jungle, was Marie Galante.

At the sight of Sexton Blake and Tinker she screamed. Half-a-dozen shots came ploughing along the jetty, and the blacks who were still there sprang on board. The ropes wore thrown off, and the rattle of the auxiliary engine sounded. Blake and Tinker tore along the jetty at top speed, reckless of the bullets that whistled about them. They took the rail in one flying leap and then, with weapons drawn, rushed full in among the blacks.

The woman uttered a terrible cry of rage, and the engine raced as the schooner began to drag hard. One of the ropes had not cleared the post, and the vessel was held. Marie Galante ran herself to cut it, and then she stood rigid, watching while a body of uniformed men came pouring down the steps from the wine shop.

They were the mounted flying squad of troopers sent by the jefe at Guitterez's urgent request. The negroes did not attempt to beat them off. The uniforms had told them that it would be useless, and they allowed themselves to be herded back on to the jetty.

But not so the woman. She fought like a tigress, biting and clawing with such fury that it took half a dozen troopers to control her. Blake and Tinker took no part in that. They couldn't bring themselves to do so. But as soon as the vessel was warped back against the jetty, they descended to the saloon to find Rymer. He was locked in a cabin where he lay bound, hand and foot, on a bunk. He said nothing when Blake cut his bonds and helped him to get up. He waited until they were on deck, then he said curtly:

"How did you know?"

"Miss Trent came and heard the fighting. Then she told me."

"I thought so. What have they done with that spitfire, Marie?"

"I fancy they have carried her into the wine shop."

"I—what's that?"

Rymer broke off to point towards the town. The whole place had sprung into sudden illumination, and down on the still air there came to them the growing volume of hoarse cries. Then followed the boom of a cannon, accompanied by the smart rattle of musketry.

"Listen," said Blake. They were silent for a few moments; then: "Do you hear that? Do you know what name they are shouting?"

"I can't make out," muttered Rymer.

"They are acclaiming Ruiz Mendoza as president. So much for your plot, Rymer. He goes into power to-night under different auspices. If I were you I think I should get back to Mary Trent. She needs you and, I fancy, wants you."

Rymer swung on him swiftly.

"I'm going now. I owe you no thanks. You have released me from the clutches of that devil, Marie; but you have ruined my game. So we are quits."

"Yes, we are quits," agreed Blake.

Then Rymer climbed over the side, and went up the steps into the wine shop.

"We don't want his thanks," said Tinker. "We did that for Mary Trent."

"You've said it, young 'un. Let's get back to the plaza and see what is going on."

The square was a dense mass of people. The whole population of Santa Marta seemed to be there. Blake and Tinker managed, after some time, to push their way near enough to the steps of the cathedral to see and hear.

On the platform at the top, stood Ruiz Mendoza, bare-headed and smiling in response to the cheers of the crowd—a fickle crowd, if you will.

And, off to one side, quite alone and looking adorably shy and sweet, was Carlotta, her eyes fixed on Ruiz with a look that held a great, wonderful love. Even Tinker took notice of it, for he whispered:

"Look at her, guv'nor! She doesn't see anyone else but him. You have done it this time."

"Shut up—he's going to speak." So Tinker subsided.

And, lifting his hand for silence, Ruiz did speak. He made a splendid, manly, impromtu speech which carried every soul in the crowd with him.

He spoke not too long, and just before he finished, he turned to Carlotta, and, before she could grasp what he was to do, he had her hand and was leading her forward. Everyone in the crowd knew the beautiful Senorita Alvarez, and that she was the daughter of Don Fernando whom everyone respected.

The gesture was enough for them. They did not wait to hear Ruiz tell them that it was through her that he stood there. They took it that he intended to announce his betrothal to the beautiful girl, and that pleased their Latin sense of romance.

They huzzaed loud and long, and the blushing Carlotta could do nothing but smile shyly and bow. As for Ruiz, he looked exalted, for he seemed to guess that when he did get a chance to ask Carlotta a certain question, she would not say "no."

Blake and Tinker returned to the Guitterez mansion, where they found the president-elect being entertained by Guitterez and his friends. Carlotta had discreetly retired. It was dawn before Blake, Tinker and Ruiz returned to the hotel, and on the way Blake told the young man what he thought he ought to know about Rymer. Of Mary he only spoke in the highest terms.

Ruiz's face clouded.

"I am sorry," he said simply. "I owe so much to him. It was he who brought me here—who put the idea in my head. And Miss Trent, she was very good to me. I must do something for him; I can't drop him cold."

"That, I should think, would be a fine action," agreed Blake.

By noon the next day they had news from San Jose that old Don Fernando had taken the bit between his teeth, and, after receiving a long telegram from his brother-in-law telling him of what had happened in Santa Marta, and that the son of old Don Ruiz was a worthy president, had gathered his supporters together, and from the steps of the cathedral had thundered out a denunciation of Don Cristofo—reading aloud his proof from the documents which Sexton Blake had placed in his hands.

There was no staying the frenzy of determination which followed. The old Government was thrown out with scarcely a shot being fired, and telegrams were received saying that Don Cristofo and his son had fled. Two days later they were captured, trying to steal past Santa Marta in a small, well-equipped sea-going motor boat.

And when the thousands of dollars loot, which Don Cristofo was taking with him, had been retrieved, he was sent on his way.

Three days after the upheaval in Santa Marta, Blake and Tinker travelled to San Jose with the new president and his party. Don Jose and, of course, Carlotta were among the members, and Blake and Tinker stood, this time, on Ruiz's right hand when, on the steps of the ancient cathedral, he was sworn in by Don Fernando as President of the Republic of Santa Marta.

And, following that impressive ceremony, they witnessed the public betrothal of the now president to Senorita Carlotta Alvarez. It was a wonderful time that followed, and Tinker hadn't recovered by the time they were back on the coast. The wedding was to be hurried forward, but they could not remain for it.

It was five days after the crash of all his plans that Huxton Rymer left Dos Hermanos on board a ship bound for Colon. Mary was feeling sad because he was miserable. She had forgiven what had happened in Santa Marta, for she realised now that he had been driven to desperate measures.

She was sitting close to him on deck, trying to comfort him, and impatient for the ship to get away, when a man in the uniform of the Santa Martan army came along the deck. He stood before them and, bowing, presented a package to Mary; following this by handing an envelope to Rymer.

"With the compliments of his Excellency, Don Ruiz Mendoza, President of the Republic," he said formally.

Mary opened her package wonderingly. When the contents were revealed she gave a gasp of delight, for before her lay a magnificent diamond and pearl pendant, together with a card from Ruiz, which said:

"Dear Miss Trent: Please accept this small gift as a token of the abiding esteem and friendship of—Yours ever sincerely,

"(Signed) Ruiz MENDOZA."

Mary turned to Rymer, who was looking down at the magnificent gift.

"It was nice of him," she said softly.

"Yes, Mary, he is a decent fellow."

"What is in your envelope?" she asked.

Rymer tore it open and took out a letter in which was enclosed a bearer draft on London for five thousand pounds. Mary gave another gasp when she saw the amount; then she eagerly took the brief letter from Rymer and read:

"Dear Professor Butterfield: I feel that some substantial material recognition is due to you for what you did towards my election to the presidency of Santa Marta. Therefore I beg of you to accept the enclosed with the very best wishes and assurances of my friendship.—Yours very sincerely,

"(Signed) Ruiz MENDOZA."

"You will keep it, won't you?" said Mary coaxingly. "He would be very hurt if you didn't."

Suddenly Rymer smiled, all his ill humour vanishing in that moment.

"Sure I'll keep it," he said. "It was we who gave him to them, wasn't it?"

Which, in litoral fact, was correct.

*   *   *   *   *

At that same moment an auxiliary schooner slid along among the green isles of the Caribbean. On the day following her attempt to kidnap Rymer, Marie Galante had been put aboard her schooner and sent down the river to the sea. For days she had paced the deck, caring not in what direction the schooner went.

But this day she was in her cabin, the door locked and the porthole covered. She lay on her bunk, clutching at the clothes as the wild passion which had been seething in her for days reached its crisis. It came in a terrible storm. It caught her in convulsions that seemed as if they must annihilate her before they passed.

At last, however, they lessened, and she lay prone, drifting on the face of a dim sea which was lit only by the flame of her passion for the man she would have dragged into the jungle with her—whom she

123

would have had to share the terrible mysteries of Voodoo, of which she was the arch-priestess.

The End.
[51100 words]

REPUBLICAN SWINDLES.
<u>Our Magazine Corner.</u>

The two chief industries of some of the smaller but very quick-living South American States seem to be revolutions and graft. There is something in the air of those republican regions that makes honesty of much less account than sudden wealth— and the rapidity with which fortunes and estates change hands there is startling and staggering.

But not one of those hectic little States has ever pulled off such a gigantic swindle as once set New York screaming for the blood of its political "bosses." It was in connection with Tammany Hall in its notorious stages, when those who ran the ring of crooks who were Tammany Hall—including the then Mayor of New York, one, Fernando Wood—fairly set that great continent rocking with the enormity of the sums of money which they scooped out of the public purse.

Faked contracts and huge percentages on all contracts given out to firms undertaking work for the Republic were their great stand-by. The story of the rise and fall of that, superbly cheeky and daring ring of crooks is too long to tell here, but the extent of their malpractices, whilst occupying positions of high honour and public trust, can be gauged from one simple fact—that one of the swindlers AMASSED twelve million dollars in five short years!

More recent times have seen the exposure of an electioneering scandal in Pennsylvania, in which £300,000 was handed out by way of bare-faced bribery by the three contestants for election to a seat in the United States Senate. Workers in the election cause were engaged wholesale, at a rate per hour which made many of them rich for life. They lined up for their pay, at regular intervals, in long queues; and before the pay-out money was fetched from the banks each of the bags containing it were carefully provided with tear-bombs, for the public were beginning to fancy taking a hand in the big game! There was only one correct way of opening the bags of bullion, and many faulty ways, any one of which meant the gassing of the unauthorised swindler!

The Big Republic has another little stunt on hand—at least, its mighty bands of swindlers have. This is the wholesale buying of convicts' releases. The world's newspapers claim for Chicago the ominous title of the world's wickedest city, chiefly on account of the fact that at least ten times as many murders occur in that city as in London. Murderers on purchased parole, and life convicts whom friends have managed to set free after only a few months in gaol, swarm in that city like flies.

Lawyers and M.P.'s are freely accused by the law-abiding citizens of Chicago of asking for, and taking, fees of anything from £200 up to £1000 for securing the unconditional release of prison scum justly condemned to lengthy incarceration by properly impanelled juries. One convict who was unable to raise sufficient "dough" to get his release from prison in this unconventional way declared that the lawyers and others who made this form of swindle their living generally reckoned to have their victims murdered as soon as possible after release, in order that evidence should not be brought against those who worked the illegal liberation.

When a millionaire stood his trial some time ago in the U.S.A. his helpers—a comprehensive word, that!—required a suite of forty rooms in the chief hotel of the town, simply to house them. Apparently the day was to be carried by sheer weight of numbers. But these sensations tread on the heels of one another unceasingly in Uncle Sam's Republic, for shortly after that big affair, one of America's notorious oil-swindlers was run in on a charge involving a £400,000 fraud.

Prohibition accounts for an enormous multitude of astounding exposures in connection with swindling in high places. The unhappy enforcement officers have estimated that 95 per cent of smuggled liquor gets into the country without being spotted, and that profits from the boot-legging business in New York alone tot up to the respectable sum of £720,000,000 a year!

The courts are reckoned to be at least two years in arrears with the trying of cases brought by the prohibition agents, fresh arrests are being made at the rate of about 400 per month. Juries are bribed freely, the heads of the crime trusts and bootlegging gangs hobnob openly with judges—and so America continues to "beat the band" where wholesale and almost unbelievable swindling is concerned.

But Germany has decided not to be outdone. As a young republic, it has much headway to make. Quite a number of successful barristers, and others officially connected with the courts of justice in Berlin, were arrested recently on a charge of trying to push Germany well into the front rank of big republican swindles.

The formal accusation was that they had formed a ring to secure the acquittal of prisoners by the simple "manipulation" of written evidence in the possession of the courts. In the criminal underworld it went by the name of the Acquittal Organisation, on appeal to which—with the necessary backing of big money—any accusative document could be "pinched" from the court archives!

---

[1] 'Sherbet' this is the most explicit reference to an intimate relationship in these stories that this editor has seen so far!/drf 2019-04-23

www.ingramcontent.com/pod-product-compliance
Lightning Source LLC
Chambersburg PA
CBHW052149170626
46812CB00004B/1660